(
and Snowball Fights

A novella

By Sarah-Jane Fraser

For Gus.

For always letting me put my cold toes
under your legs to warm up,
for giving me your hoody when I'm
freezing...
and for supporting my dreams.

Acknowledgements

With massive thanks to my wonderful team of beta readers, I could never do this without you! Hannah Ellis, Lisa West, Gillian Baxter, Alexandra O'Malley, Karen Champion, Kathryn Fraser and Cara Archer you are all stars and I appreciate you so much.

Lots of thanks to the wonderful support of the lovely people at ChickLitChatHQ, with particular thanks to Kirsty McManus. Huge thanks to Carina Christensen for your fabulous insight.

To my friends at Yatton Library Writers Club, thank you for your honest feedback on readouts and for always being a positive support. I always enjoy the opportunities you give me to write out of my comfort zone.

Thanks to my followers on my Facebook author page and Twitter for all your support and for choosing the name of our gorgeous leading male.

Table of Contents

Chapter one.

Nancy twirled her curly auburn hair around her finger while she listened to the ringing tone, waiting for her best friend to pick up.

"Hi Nancy, long time no hear!" answered Tessa's sing-song voice.

"Hi, how are you? I miss you!" Nancy clutched the receiver tightly as if hugging the phone would be as good as hugging her friend.

"I'm great, how are you doing?"

"I'm good," she hesitated. "I have some time off work, I wondered if we could meet for a good ol' catch up?"

"When?"

"Next week?"

"I'd love to but I'm away with work," Tessa replied, a note of disappointment in her voice.

"Oh, that's a shame, are you doing anything fun?"

"I have a conference in Denmark."

"Oooh, that'll be lovely this time of year."

"It's January, it'll be cold," Tessa replied pragmatically. "You know what, how much time off do you have? You should come too!"

"No, I couldn't... Could I?"

"Of course! I'm out during the days, but we'd have the evenings and the weekend at the end. You could spend the days exploring or chilling out. You just need to sort out a flight."

"But where would I stay?"

"You can stay in my hotel room, it'll be like we're back at uni again. Please say yes."

Nancy pursed her lips thinking of a reason not to go, but desperate not to find one. She really needed to get away from everything and spend some quality time with her friend.

"Yes!" she called out, "Yes, I'll come but only if you're sure."

***

Nancy stepped out of the aeroplane onto the rickety staircase and an icy blast of freezing air slapped her in the face. She pulled her scarf round closer and bowing her head into the wind carefully descended, toting her carry-on luggage behind her. She knew it was going to be cold in Denmark but it still took her breath away.

It was a relief to get out of the elements and in to the terminal building.

Nancy followed the crowd, eventually coming through the arrivals gate. She was bundled into by a whirlwind of arms, legs and dark hair.

"You're here, you're here," cried Tessa.

Squeezing her tight and then holding her out at arms-length, Nancy said, "You're a sight for sore eyes."

"I can't believe you came!"

"I can't believe I'm here!" Nancy replied.

A tall figure stepped up to them and coughed.

"Torben Christensen," he said and stuck his hand out to Nancy.

"Nancy Clarke," she replied automatically, finding herself shaking hands with a Norse god.

"Oh yeah, this is Torben," said Tessa. "He works with me at Danglish. He gave me a lift here to get you."

Nancy studied Torben; she was struck by his piercing blue eyes, she smiled and started to thank him but he interrupted. "Are you ready to go?" he asked grumpily. "These airport lights are giving me a headache."

As they walked to the car, Nancy linked arms with Tessa and leaned in to say, "Are you sure it's ok I'm here?" Paranoia and doubt tried to creep in, but Nancy was determined to leave the negativity back at home.

"Of course, it's the best thing ever! Nearly everyone's brought their wives or partners. It's cool."

"Phew!" said Nancy and then as an after-thought she asked, "Oh god, are they gonna think that I'm *with* you, that I'm a WAG?!"

"Maybe," laughed Tessa, "but it won't matter, I work with a very open-minded bunch."

Nancy nodded towards Torben and whispered, "He doesn't seem too happy that I'm here."

"Hmmm, he's the exception to the rule," Tessa replied quietly. "He's not happy with anything. Ever. He's so grumpy, after we arrived a couple of nights ago he made us walk around for twenty minutes until we found a bar with the right ambience." Tessa rolled her eyes at the memory.

With an eyebrow slightly raised, Nancy studied him from behind, he had broad shoulders and his long legs marched him determinedly forward. She wondered why on earth he had offered to give her a lift if he was as grumpy as Tessa had said. "Let's crack on, best not annoy him anymore," she said as she picked up the pace.

The two women scuttled along giggling and trying to run whilst still linking arms. They fell into the back of the car while Torben watched on. They didn't see the flicker of amusement that crossed his face as he shut the door.

It was already dark and Nancy rested her head on the window and watched the glow of the lights from cars and buildings whizz by. She loved the little glimpses into other people's lives you got as the lit windows flashed past; dioramas of daily life.

The road darkened and Torben drove them out into the wilderness.

"Where are we going?" asked Nancy.

"The hotel we're all staying at is in the middle of nowhere," said Tessa begrudgingly. "There're just endless fields and farmland which basically means there's nothing to do."

"It sounds idyllic," said Nancy.

"It is," said Torben.

"At least the conference is back in the city, there's a bit more going on there, but it's no Copenhagen," said Tessa with a sigh.

After about twenty minutes the hotel came into sight; a huge, old Danish manor house. Bright yellow in colour and crowned with a peaked grey roof. Hundreds of little square windows with cute sash bars dividing them into quarters like in a picture book adorned the fascia.

Torben swung the car onto the drive and dropped them off at the front. "I'll see you at dinner," he called out in response to their thanks.

With breath puffing out in clouds in front of them, they tottered into the lobby.

"Ahhhhh that's better," said Tessa, embracing the warmth that hit them.

"Brrrrr," said Nancy, "I know you said it would be cold but… wow!"

The bell boy insisted on relieving Nancy of her carry-on suitcase and she smiled gratefully.

Tessa said, "Tak," to thank him and directed him up to their room.

"I really need to learn to speak some Danish," she said, "but I think I can remember that."

"You tend to pick up a bit," said Tessa, "working for a half Danish company."

The concierge offered them some steaming mugs which they took gratefully, clutching them to their chests like comforters.

"Mmmm, is this mulled wine?" said Nancy.

"Yeah similar, it's called gløgg," said Tessa. She used a teaspoon to scoop up some sultanas and skinny flakes of almonds from the bottom. "This is the best bit," she said with a grin and spooned the tasty morsels in to her mouth.

"Let's get toasty over there," Nancy suggested, nodding towards a roaring open fire at the edge of the foyer. "So, how's the conference going?" She asked once they had settled in to a cosy seat.

"Not bad, learning a lot and... I've kind of met someone."

"Here? That's exciting! How?"

"Well, I've known him through work for a while but I never saw him much so nothing had ever happened... until now."

"You don't waste any time."

"I never did," replied Tessa with laughter in her voice and her eye brow raised.

"True," said Nancy casting her mind back to their time at university. Tessa used to go through men like ice lollies on a hot summer's day- guzzling them quickly and then casting any debris aside before it got messy. Nancy was more of a home-made Christmas cake kind of person when it came to relationships; slow baking; feeding it gradually before taking a bite when the time was right. "What's his name? What's he like?" The questions tumbled out with her enthusiasm.

"He's called Neil." Tessa couldn't stop the grin stretching across her face. "You can meet him later, he's staying here too."

"I'm not gonna be cramping your style, am I?" Nancy got hit by another pang of concern, she didn't usually jump on aeroplanes and charge around the world without thinking it through.

"No, not at all. I invited you," Tessa reassured her. "Plus, it's early days, I'd rather catch up with you."

7

"Well, I look forward to meeting him. Maybe I'll grill him and ask him what his intentions are," Nancy said, giggling.

Tessa batted her hand at her and tutted. "So, how's everything with you?" she asked.

Nancy gave a tight smile and looked sideways at her. "Yeah, everything's good."

"Really?" asked Tessa, not sounding convinced.

"No, it's really great."

"Hmmmm," said Tessa. "Ok, if you're sure."

"What? Everything's fantastic."

"You should have stopped at good, I definitely don't believe you now. Still, we've got a few days, I'll get it out of you eventually."

Nancy shifted uneasily in her seat and muttered, "Everything's fine."

Chapter two.

"That is one hella ugly sweater!" stated Tessa as Nancy walked out of the bathroom.

"What, you don't like it?" Nancy smoothed her hands over the thick knit, as Tessa looked her up and down.

"Well, firstly, it's January and that is most definitely a *Christmas* jumper."

"I like to think of it as a winter jumper."

"And, well, the snow flakes and Christmas trees really frame the giant deer head motif, don't get me wrong. I just think the pink clashes a bit with the red, white, blue and green."

Nancy looked in the long mirror on the door. "I see your point..."

"But you're gonna wear it anyway?"

"Yep!" said Nancy and she laughed as Tessa shook her head in exasperation.

Tessa was wearing a short black dress and sheer tights, with a conservative (for Tessa) three-inch heel.

Nancy surveyed her counterpart and said, "You look nice, like, really nice. Do I need to be dressier?"

"No, it's just a team meal in the hotel

dining room. You could go in your pyjamas if you want."

"Don't tempt me. So how come you're all dressed up? Is it because *Neil's* going to be there?"

Tessa's outfit suddenly became accessorised by some very blushed cheeks.

"There's no harm in looking nice," she replied curtly.

Nancy started clutching her heart and sighing, "Mmmm, Neeeeeeil!"

There was a knock at the door and Tessa was quick to open it, while Nancy was still prancing around, teasing her.

"Did I hear my name?" asked a deep voice.

Eyes as wide as an owl, Nancy whipped her head round and stared at the door. Silhouetted in the door frame was a well built, dark haired man, his olive complexion contrasted beautifully with Tessa's lily-white skin.

"Hi, Neil," said Tessa. "Nancy-Neil, Neil- Nancy."

All Nancy could do was exclaim, "Eeep!" She flicked her wayward curls off her face and composed herself as she walked over to the door to greet him. "Nice to meet you."

"And you," replied Neil, his brown eyes twinkling mischievously. "Shall we head down?"

The three of them made their way

down to the big dining area. They walked into a sea of people chatting and laughing, to Nancy it seemed like everyone knew everyone.

"Wow," she whispered into Tessa's ear. "Are all these people at the conference?"

"Half of them, and then there's all the plus ones. See, I told you it was ok to come." She smiled warmly at Nancy and squeezed her hand.

Neil went off to find them some drinks and Tessa watched him walk away with a dreamy look on her face.

"I haven't seen you look like that since Chris Jenkins in the second year," said Nancy.

"Hmmm?" Tessa came out of her reverie. "So, what do you think?"

"He seems nice so far, I mean, he's getting us drinks- what more could a girl want?"

Tessa just nodded, not really listening. "He's lush, isn't he? He's just so much fun, and that body... I could eat him up. Do you think his ears are burning? Us talking about him?"

"Not as much as my face was when he busted me messing around in our room!"

"Mmmmm," said Tessa and was lost again, gazing after him.

Nancy looked around and took in the gaggle of people they'd be dining with; there were maybe fifty in all. There were people of all ages, shapes and sizes and more than enough winter woolly jumpers to put her at ease about her wardrobe choice.

Neil came back with three proseccos and after they all clinked glasses he immediately engaged Tessa in a full recap of the day's events at the conference. Nancy smiled and nodded along but had absolutely no idea what they were chatting about.

She carried on people watching and caught sight of Torben stood by the bar. He towered above most people there; a Viking in a sea of Celts. She gave a small wave but he had turned and started talking to someone in a suit that had just approached him. Resigning herself to being a gooseberry for the foreseeable future she tried to tune back into the conversation but they had moved on to talking about someone called Jakob at the office. Nancy fixed a smile on her face and tried to look enthralled.

***

Catherine Lang liked to talk. Nancy was sandwiched between Catherine, who was chewing her ear off, and Tessa, who was effectively ignoring her as she hung off Neil's every word.

She tried to catch Torben's attention. He

was sat a few places along the table but he was in deep conversation with the person next to him and hadn't seemed to notice. Nancy was entranced by his Nordic good looks, he reminded her of a sexy vampire she'd seen on TV; all blond and brooding.

Turning to Catherine, Nancy said, "Have you been away on a conference with your husband before?"

This triggered another monologue. She smiled and nodded through a fish soup starter, frikadeller meatballs for main course and an apple strudel style dessert. Catherine Lang's constant stream of chatter was unrelenting; Nancy was struggling to keep track of it all.

As Nancy polished off the last of the flaky pastry and cranberry coulis, Catherine drew breath and said, "And that's why I'm so pleased to have met you, you must come to our infamous after-dinner games party."

She coughed on a crumb as she vaguely concurred, "Mmmmhmmm."

Swallowing hard she wondered what on earth she had agreed to.

There was a tinkling noise from the top of the room and everyone's attention was drawn to the head waiter tapping a wine glass with a spoon. "Ladies and gentlemen, please join us for coffee and petits fours by the fire."

As they filed out of the grand dining room, Nancy wondered how they would all fit in the small entrance foyer, but they didn't go to the fire that she had warmed herself by when they arrived. They turned a corner and went through an arch shrouded with a thick velvet curtain. The head of a deer with magnificent antlers was mounted above it, and Nancy felt her winter jumper was more appropriate than ever.

They entered a cavernous room. It was the perfect space for their large group; there were lots of plump chairs and low tables dotted around. Her gaze was drawn to a huge hearth with a hearty fire roaring inside it. Across the back wall was a long bar with fairy lights twinkling along the edge; a mirror over the mantelpiece reflected the gorgeous lights around the room. The couple of glasses of wine Nancy had with dinner made everything look shiny.

Catherine grabbed her arm and before she knew it she found herself embroiled in a game of team Scrabble.

"I'm with Nancy and George," announced Catherine. George Lang was Catherine's husband, and as far as Nancy could tell, he hadn't uttered a single word all evening. Leaning close Catherine said, "This is a bit of a tradition, we always play it. Just remember there are no Q's or W's in Danish Scrabble."

"But I only know 'Tak'," said Nancy, a note of concern in her voice.

"Oh no, dear, we're not playing *Danish* Scrabble, just with the Danish board."

"Ohhhh," she replied, breathing a sigh of relief.

George caught her eye and said, "Just do what Cath says and you'll be fine." He winked at Nancy and then resumed his silence.

"Now, it's best if you introduce yourself to anyone you don't know," said Catherine. "It's what we do when we're in Denmark."

Looking around at the gathering Nancy swallowed hard, she knew instantly that she wouldn't know anyone. With Catherine nodding encouragingly she stuck out her hand and went around the group shaking everyone's hand. She was surprised by the friendly, welcoming hand-shakes she got back. After the first couple, she didn't even find it awkward, although her hand was aching from the vigorous shakes. She did her best to remember as many names as possible but only Jakob and Carina stuck in her head.

"Let's get started then," announced Catherine, clearly the leader.

Nancy found her love of reading came in particularly handy when thinking of vocabulary that didn't have Q's or W's, and she and the Langs were making a great team. There was plenty of friendly banter with the other teams and the overwhelming feelings of being an outsider when she had first walked into the dining hall were soon starting to fade.

In a moment where the opposition were taking a particularly long time to play their tiles, Nancy decided to head to the bar for a refill. Torben was there, half sat on a stool, his long legs propping himself on the floor. He was staring deeply out the window, a tumbler of whiskey balanced between his thumb and finger.

"Hi," said Nancy, placing herself in his field of vision.

"Oh, errr, hi" he replied, brusquely.

"Sorry to disturb you," she said, matching his tone. "I just wondered if you fancied a drink or wanted to join the game?"

Torben surveyed the boisterous group surrounding the board game and then said, "No thanks."

"Please yourself," she replied.

Nancy sighed to herself as she noted that Tessa and Neil were huddled cosily in a corner and the only person she knew, other than the Langs, was being an obnoxious git.

Heading back to the group, she got a welcome cheer and Nancy felt more settled than she had all evening.

"Nancy, it's your turn," said Carina, as Nancy sat back down.

With a new-found confidence, she managed to turn her team's unfortunate collection of a G, a Y and a Z into a triple word scoring "zygote".

While Nancy was celebrating her team's win at the bar Torben looked over to the rowdy group to see if he could get Nancy on her own again. She had surprised him earlier by popping up so suddenly and he realised he must have come over as rude. She was chatting away with Catherine Lang who seemed to only be pausing to give George orders. Reluctant to get waylaid by the venerable Mrs Lang, he decided to leave her to it. However, his eyes lingered; he couldn't stop looking at all the different shades of red and brown that were glinting off her glossy locks, reflecting the fire's glow.

Chapter three.

When Tessa bowled into their room that night Nancy was already fast asleep, so it pained her to get up so early and in the pitch black in order to catch the staff bus to the conference. She scribbled a note for Nancy before she left, placing it next to her on her pillow.

Nancy awoke to find herself alone in the room, she squinted into the morning light and drowsily rolled onto her side away for the brightness creeping around the edge of the curtains. Something crackled under her face. Startled, she was now fully alert.

N, Fancy meeting me for a drink
at the microbrewery when I've finished today?
There's a great shopping mall in the city,
some good cafes and you can even do a
bike tour. I know you love cycling.
See you at 6, T xx

Nancy smiled; she did love a bike tour and as Denmark was notoriously flat she thought that it would be a very good way to spend her first day.

"Right, best get ready and head out for the day," she said to herself.

She swept the curtains back and squinted. No wonder the light was so bright, outside it was glowing white. Snow. Everywhere. Nancy gave a little jump with joy and hurried to get her snow boots. It crossed her mind that the bike tour might not be such fun, but the city would look beautiful. Messing around in the snow would be a very welcome distraction.

***

The microbrewery was starting to fill up with people meeting up after work. Nancy had snagged the last available table in the window and looked out at the bustling street along the canal. She had a lovely view of the multi-coloured buildings and town houses lining the waterfront; it was stunning, like an image from a travel guide. The icing of snow on the rooftops made it even more enchanting.

A familiar shape walked passed; tall and stepping determinedly. Caught up in the friendly atmosphere Nancy found herself waving.

Torben, quite distracted thinking about the day's discussions was surprised to find Nancy grinning and waving at him through a slightly steamy window. He found himself opening the door and heading over to her.

"Hej," he said.

"Hej," Nancy responded to his greeting, trying to copy his pronunciation.

Torben didn't know what he was doing there, he had been drawn in by the cosy hubbub and the unexpected and animated welcome. He didn't always get beautiful women smiling and waving at him. He suddenly found himself lost for words.

"Have you had a good day?" asked Nancy.

Torben hesitated, he was never very good at small talk, he found he never knew if people were actually interested in his day or not. He decided to play it safe and just said, "Yes, thank you."

"Would you like to join me?" asked Nancy. "I'm just waiting for Tessa."

Nancy didn't notice his face darken slightly.

"I wouldn't want to ruin your plans with your friend."

"You wouldn't be and you'd be keeping me company while I wait for her."

"Ok, thank you," he said and sat down in the chair opposite her. "I won't outstay my welcome once Tessa arrives though."

"Don't be silly. Tessa should be along any minute. Do you want a drink while we wait?"

"Can you recommend any?" asked Torben. The microbrewery wasn't his usual place to go when he was in the city, it was new and usually stuck with what he knew.

Nancy laughed. "I've not been here long enough to try them all yet. Oh look, they do a beer flight sampling board. Let's get that and try them all."

"Ok," said Torben. He found his mood lifting with her enthusiasm.

As they waited for the beer flight, Torben was surprised to find himself easily chatting away with Nancy. He had just asked her about her day as the waitress delivered a long teak board with 5 circles grooved out of it, each with a small glass slotted inside. Varying shades of amber shone out at them.

They selected a glass each and tinked their glasses together.

"Skål," said Torben. "It's Danish for cheers."

"Skål!" replied Nancy.

"You were telling me about your day?"

"Oh yes, after I saw the cathedral I went to the museum and then after lunch, I went to the modern art gallery. It was fabulous."

"You've been busy. How did you manage to do so much?"

"I hired a bike. I wasn't going to because of the snow, but then when I saw that the roads and paths were cleared, well, there was no reason not to. And besides, I felt like a local cycling around everywhere."

Torben smiled and said, "You like to cycle?"

Nancy nodded enthusiastically and said, "I don't normally cycle back in London, I'm too scared of getting knocked off."

Suddenly the smile on Torben's face fell. Nancy followed his line of sight and saw Tessa walking over to them.

"Drink up, we're going," she said by way of a greeting.

"Hi. What? No, we've just got these."

"I've got us a table booked at a swanky new bar. If we aren't there by seven we'll lose it."

"But it's only..." Nancy looked at her watch. "Oh, it's a quarter to, I've got no idea where the evening's gone."

"You don't mind do you, Torben?" said Tessa, not really caring about his answer.

"No, you ladies go ahead."

"But it's so early and we haven't finished our drinks," said Nancy.

Tessa grabbed two of the glasses and downed one and then the other. "You can manage that last one, can't you, Torben?"

"Er, yes, but..."

"Good. Come on, Nancy, my feet are killing me and if we don't get to the bar in time I'll have to stand up all night. Come on," she said, tugging at her elbow.

Flustered, Nancy found herself being dragged away.

"Sorry about this," she said to Torben. "Thanks for keeping me company..."

"My pleasure," replied Torben but Nancy had already been swallowed into the crowd.

Outside Tessa slowed down and let go of Nancy's arm.

"Phew, that's got rid of him," said Tessa.

"What? Why have you dragged me away, that was so rude."

"Don't be silly, it's only Torben. How did you get lumbered with him anyway?"

"I wasn't lumbered with him, I'd invited him to join us."

"Oh, thank God we ditched him when we did, that would have been a fun killer. Come on, seriously, I don't want to lose this table."

Tessa turned a corner and led Nancy into a loud bar. Shouting over the bass and mainly relying on lip reading Nancy realised she wouldn't be able to do much talking. They were soon joined by Neil, Carina, Jakob and some of the other people at the conference. Nancy put on a broad smile as her heart fell a little bit more; they definitely wouldn't be able to do any catching up tonight.

***

Torben took off his belt and tie and loosened his collar. Kicking his shoes off under the table, he flopped backwards onto his bed. His elbows stuck out as he tucked his hands behind his head.

This is unexpected, he thought to himself. He puffed out his cheeks and exhaled slowly.

He considered his two-year-long irritation with Tessa. Since she literally bounced in to the office a couple of years ago they had tolerated each other but that was it. Working at the same company closely together they had to rub along and get on, but that didn't mean they particularly liked each other. However, the culture of working for Danglish meant he felt an almost big brotherly affection for her; she was like an annoying little sister. Tessa often wound him up with her loud, brash ways; he considered her a spoilt princess, a diva, and never expected to have anything in common with her. Until Nancy.

His face softened and a smile played across his lips. Nancy was so different. He couldn't understand how the two women were friends, they seemed poles apart. She kept surprising him and popping up suddenly, she set him on edge. But in a good way.

If he hadn't felt that familial duty to help Tessa collect her friend from the airport, they would never have met. Perhaps having Tessa as a 'little sister' wasn't such a bad thing after all. Maybe he should cut her a little slack.

Yes, he thought to himself, this is all very unexpected.

Chapter four.

Nancy awoke to find Tessa wildly tossing things out of the wardrobe and onto the end of her bed.

"Morning," she said with a croak.

"I'm running late and I can't find my lucky red top," replied Tessa.

"I think it's in the drawer. I remember seeing something red yesterday."

"Phew!" said Tessa as she tore it open and pulled the sweater frantically over her head. "See you tonight," she called over her shoulder as she ran out of the room.

Nancy sat up, rubbing the sleep out of her eyes. She took in the fact that it was almost eight thirty and that Tessa's pillow hadn't been slept on in one glance and sunk back down. Tessa and Neil had carried on drinking in the hotel bar when they'd got back in the night before. Nancy was pleased she had stopped drinking when she did-she already had a thumping head. It was only the call of coffee and the fear of missing breakfast that eventually prised her out of bed and into the shower.

She felt a little nervous heading back down to the dining room alone, she hadn't

27

socialised with any of the people staying at the hotel without having a drink in hand. It was empty when she arrived and she helped herself to a much needed, large, americano coffee. Her stomach grumbled and she scanned the breakfast buffet. Her eyes fell on a basket of Danish pastries, there was a little board in front with the word "wienerbrød" on. She chuckled as she realised that Danish pastries would be called something completely different in Denmark. They looked delicious so she grabbed one and went to sit by the window; gazing out at the snowy scene.

There was a little chapel perched on top of a nearby hill that Nancy could see from her spot. Needing some alone time, she decided to hike to it; this would give her the perfect opportunity to get her head around her situation. She hoped that then when she got a chance to talk properly with Tessa, she could get a new take on it all too. Perhaps then she'd know what to do.

One by one, other wives and girlfriends joined her and she found herself amongst a gaggle of chattering women. Overwhelmed by all the talking, Nancy stayed mute. With her own troubles niggling at her she struggled to follow their conversation and keep her thoughts straight amongst all the chaos.

Once Nancy had finished her breakfast she smiled politely and said, "See you later," as she left.

Catherine caught her eye and smiled but didn't break from her constant stream of chatter to one of the other wives.

Nancy arranged with the concierge for a packed lunch to be made for her and went up to the room to retrieve her snow boots. She laced them carefully in the foyer and then headed out on her little adventure, her lunch stowed in her back pack. She was ready to do some serious thinking.

As she took her first steps onto the untouched snow a smile crept across her face; the squeak and crunch of walking on snow always made her feel happy. She settled into a slow, plodding rhythm as she made her way up the winding path.

***

Tessa flew out of the bedroom in panic and headed back down to the reception.

"She's not here," she yelled at Neil. "Where is she?!"

"Is she in the bar?" he asked, a lost look on his face.

"No, you idiot, we've already checked there." Tessa massaged her temples, feebly trying to prevent a headache from setting in. It was Torben who intervened as she started shouting at the concierge. "Well, where did she say she was going? Why didn't you ask her?" she challenged, leaning aggressively over his desk.

"Tessa, calm down. What's happened?" he asked.

"Nancy's gone bloody AWOL," she replied before turning back to the concierge. "Check again," she shouted as she pointed to his notepad.

"What is this awol? Is she not well?"

"No, I mean she's disappeared. I can't find her anywhere." She thumbed in the concierge's general direction and said, "This guy hasn't seen her since this morning."

Torben spoke in quick Danish to the concierge and then turned back to Tessa.

"He said that he got her a packed lunch organised and that she had snow boots on and left in that direction." He pointed in the direction of the chapel, now invisible in the thick snow.

"Oh god, oh god..." said Tessa. "Her mum's gonna kill me."

"I can round up some of the guys, we can go out and look for her," suggested Torben. Seeing the white-out he thought that, for once, Tessa's drama may not be misplaced.

Just as he started summoning over George, Jakob and some of his other colleagues the front door blew open and in rolled Nancy, Catherine, Carina and about four other ladies. They were chatting merrily until the stony silence in the foyer drew their attention. Well, everyone's attention except Catherine's.

"And that's why I said, George, we just have to have bifold doors." She carried on talking, oblivious to the awkward situation.

"Nancy!" shrieked Tessa. "You're alive!"

"What? Of course I'm alive."

"Where the hell have you been? I've been worried sick. He told me you'd gone up there," said Tessa madly gesticulating between the flustered looking concierge and the wilderness.

"Yeah, I popped up to the little chapel up there. What's wrong with that?"

"But when you weren't here I was so worried."

"When I came back down I met this lot and they dragged me along to their pamper afternoon," explained Nancy, slightly puzzled by all the fuss.

"Jesus, Nancy, you could have told me," hissed Tessa.

"But you were at your conference. You said, 'see you tonight'. I didn't think I had to tell you my every move."

"Well... well..." said Tessa, slightly embarrassed and more than a little irritated.

"Crisis averted?" asked Torben as he cut in. "I'll see you later," he said, his

31

eyebrow raised disparagingly. He walked off briskly.

"Nothing to see here," announced Tessa to the gathering crowd.

She ushered Nancy up to their room. Nancy gave the group of pampered ladies a bemused wave as she went.

"What's got into you?" said Tessa as she shut the bedroom door behind her.

"Nothing, what's got into you," replied Nancy, slightly confused.

"Well, you can't just go off like that. I was worried."

"You can't expect me to sit around here waiting for you, that's just weird."

"You could have left a note," said Tessa.

"But you said 'see you at dinner'. Why would I leave a note, unless I wasn't going to see you at dinner?"

"We're going to be late *for* dinner now," said Tessa. She huffed as she pulled on a close fitting, royal blue dress.

Nancy ran a brush through her hair and then said, "Ready."

Tessa pulled a face, clearly unimpressed by Nancy's efforts, as she rapidly reapplied her lipstick. "No disappearing acts tonight," she ordered. "I still don't feel like we've had a proper catch up."

"I'm all yours," said Nancy, with a hopeful smile. She was desperate to have a proper talk with her best friend; she needed a hug, and some perspective.

They left the room in a flurry of perfume and headed back down to the dining room. Sat in their usual spots, Nancy found herself once again being ignored by Tessa and talked at by Catherine Lang.

***

"Absolutely not!" said Tessa, disagreeing passionately.

The people around Nancy's part of the table found themselves entangled in an argument between Tessa and Torben. Even Catherine was sat in silence as she followed it closely.

"Customers want the best, the fastest, the newest- they want immediate access. This is a 'now' culture. We need to be loud and 'in their faces' to get their attention and to keep it."

"Perhaps to get new customers, but the ones we've got don't appreciate the hard sell. We need to back off or we could end up losing them."

"That doesn't make sense, Torben, it's so boring and unexciting."

"All this technology and immediacy, it's a turn off, especially for some of the older clients. They like what they know. They like their traditions. We should respect that."

Sloshing her almost empty wine glass in his direction, Tessa stated, "Traditions are irrelevant; has-beens. They hold us back. We just don't need clients like that." She thumped her glass down heavily as if to punctuate the end of the matter.

Tentatively George said, "Well, that's what this conference is all about, it gives us a chance to explore ideas and express our opinions. What do you think Nancy?"

"Hmmm?" replied Nancy, startled.

"As an outsider- a prospective new client- what would you prefer? The hard sell or softly softly?"

"Erm, I don't think I'm the best person to ask. I don't know anything about your business."

"Then you're exactly the right person to ask," replied George. "How would you like to be approached by someone from Danglish?"

"I wouldn't", replied Nancy. The people listening chuckled, but their gaze was trained on her expectantly, wanting her to continue. "I, personally, would be a bit intimidated by the hard sell. I wouldn't want everything loud and in my face. I think I'd just shut down to it." Nancy was aware that Tessa was shaking her head in the background but she carried on. "I'd want to be asked what I wanted and have them listen to the response. So, I guess I'm on team softly softly." Nancy awkwardly gestured in Torben's direction.

George nodded appreciatively at her honesty and Torben almost cracked a smile.

"What about personality screening?" asked Catherine suddenly. "I read a magazine article in the hairdressers about it. There's software that scans a person's or a business' online presence and then deduces the best way to approach them according to their personality type."

George looked at his wife with a smile and said, "I always knew it was a good idea to bring plus ones away with us. You always get different ideas rather than only consulting the same people who are sat together in the same office all day. Now, who else has any ideas that might just be crazy enough to work?"

The awkward tension from the heated exchange was broken and everyone started talking in smaller groups again. The chink of silverware on china rang out as people got back to the meal at hand.

Using the chatty babble as a cover Nancy leaned over to Catherine and quietly asked, "What *do* they do at Danglish though?"

For the second time that night Catherine Lang was speechless. Torben definitely cracked a smile this time, having overheard Nancy's question, but he quickly turned away so no one would see.

After a long, puzzled look Catherine asked, "Do you really not know?"

Chapter five.

The fire roared and crackled. A delicious aroma of pine filled the air; someone had thrown some sprigs into the hearth, filling the room with the nostalgic scent of Christmas. Tessa was sat curled in a plump armchair while Neil perched on the edge of it regaling her with some more 'in' jokes. Nancy leaned against the wall nearby watching the blaze and clasping her hands around a mug of hot gløgg.

"You've got my usual spot," said a deep voice.

Nancy startled out of her reverie and stood bolt upright, as if she had been caught being naughty. "Oh, I'm sorry. I could move if you want."

Torben smiled. "No, I was just kidding. It's usually me propping up the fireplace."

"It's mesmerising, I was completely lost in thought."

"I didn't mean to disturb you, I just thought I saw a kindred spirit."

Nancy smiled. "How do you mean?"

He shrugged. "Fire. Gløgg. Vacant look on your face. Perhaps sneakily avoiding Catherine Lang?"

"She's very nice!" said Nancy, defensively.

"Yes, and very chatty," said Torben, laughing. "How did you manage to get out of team Scrabble tonight?"

"That'd be telling."

"At least you're not getting embroiled in any more shop talk."

"I know, it was a bit awkward disagreeing with Tessa at dinner earlier. Especially as I really know nothing about it."

Torben grinned and replied, "I think you're like me; you like to enjoy the quieter things..."

"Exactly!" Nancy paused and appraised Torben; the blue of his shirt matched the exact shade of his eyes and the kind smile on his face stirred something in her. "So, do you ever prop up the bar?" Nancy asked, cheekily.

"Absolutely," Torben replied. He held his arm out wide, indicating she should lead the way. As they walked away he asked, "Do you need to tell them where you're going?" He nodded his head towards Tessa and Neil.

"We aren't going far," said Nancy earnestly. "Plus, I don't think they'll miss me."

"They did earlier," said Torben with laughter dancing in his eyes as he gently teased her.

Nancy shook her head in disbelief. "I've had that many people checking I wasn't lost out in the snow," said Nancy, half irritated and half embarrassed. "It's nice they care I guess."

"We're a very caring bunch here, a bit like family. Have you known Tessa long?"

"Yeah, for ages- since the first year at university. We lived together."

"Ah, so you are like family too."

Nancy nodded and asked, "Do you know Neil?"

"Yes, through work."

"What's he like?"

"He's a nice guy as far as I've seen," said Torben.

"Good, so I can be happy for her."

"Yes." Looking at Nancy, Torben considered that she didn't actually look that happy.

"Let me get this round," he said. "Do you like hot chocolate?"

"Errr, yes!"

"And rum?"

"Yes... I like where this is going!"

Torben ordered their drinks and the bar man brought over two chunky mugs brimming with thick cream and a dusting of cocoa.

They clinked their mugs together and Torben said, "Skål!"

"Skål," replied Nancy. "Tak!"

"You've learnt Danish?"

"The odd word," said Nancy crossing her fingers as she hoped he didn't start testing her on it.

"Oh look, it's snowing!" said Torben suddenly. His face lit up like a kid at Christmas. More snow was falling down on what was already a solid white blanket.

"I love watching it fall, especially when I'm safe and warm inside."

"Yes, I think that's one of life's greatest pleasures," said Torben softly.

They found themselves drifting over to a snug window seat. Nancy sat entranced by the soft flurry of flakes.

Torben watched Nancy while she was engrossed. As heavy and as hard as the snow outside; he was falling for her. He couldn't stop himself. All resolve from his heartbreak six years ago was melting away; his reserved detachedness diminishing. Nancy was very different and he knew it; he could feel something tugging at him inside, pulling him towards her. He tore his eyes away and looked out of the window, he didn't want to come on too strong. He didn't want to ruin anything. Try and play it cool, Torben, he thought.

"You coming?" Tessa's voice abruptly shattered the calm contentment that was surrounding the snow gazers.

Nancy startled and looked up at Tessa blankly. "Huh?"

"You ready to go? Neil and I are heading to a club in the city, there's a taxi waiting."

"Oh, er, I don't really fancy a club right now."

"But we always go clubbing when we're together." Tessa put her hand on her hip as she stuck it out at a jaunty angle.

"I'm just not in the mood for it," said Nancy.

"So, you're not coming?"

"Er, no, I think I'll stay here."

"You want to stay here? With Torben?"

"Yes."

Tessa tutted and as she swivelled round on her toes to walk off she called out, "Suit yourself. See you tomorrow."

When Nancy turned back towards Torben she noticed a slight panicked look disappearing from his face. "Don't feel you need to babysit me though," she said quickly. "I'm not really into the clubbing scene anymore and I didn't fancy being an old crow stuck with those two love birds."

"I didn't think I was babysitting you, I'm enjoying our evening together."

"Me too. I just thought you might feel stuck with me... you looked nervous." There was a half joking, half deadly serious note to Nancy's voice. She had definitely seen him look worried.

"Not at all." Torben leaned forward

41

and tucked a stray curl of hair behind Nancy's ear. His voice deepened and he carefully said, "I was thinking that I like you very much and I don't want to blow it." His eyes held hers and she felt he could see right down into her soul. The whirl of snow outside the window seemed to slow. Nancy held her breath in the stillness. A log popped loudly in the flames and the snow started to flurry and dance again.

Had he really just said that? Nancy's mind was reeling. She tried to flirt while she composed herself. "I don't want you to blow it either," she replied cheekily. "Now, what was this?" Nancy held up her empty mug. "And how do we get another one?"

Nancy used the diversion to try and calm herself, what with her pulse racing and her breath catching, she wondered if she might actually pass out. Could you be hospitalised for swooning?

Clutching their freshly replenished mugs, they headed away from the bar and back towards the swirling snow storm.

"Do you want to go and watch it?" asked Nancy, indicating to their vacant window seat.

"We can do better than that," replied Torben. He grabbed her hand and pulled her round the back of the bar.

They passed through a 'staff only' door and Nancy felt a tingle of excitement. Fumbling in the darkness, Torben eventually found a switch and managed to click on a bare overhead bulb which zinged and illuminated the store area behind the scenes. Heading confidently across the storeroom, Torben led her over to a rickety ladder and gave her a boost up into a creaky and dark attic. It was no mean feat climbing up whilst nursing her hot chocolate.

"Where are we going?"

"You'll see," said Torben and followed her up the ladder. "I've been here many times before. But I've never shown anyone else this," he added hastily.

With a bit of a strain and a shoulder barge Torben pushed open a narrow door which led out onto a small, sheltered balcony. Rummaging in a box just inside the door he produced two thick woollen blankets and, placing his mug aside, wrapped one blanket around Nancy's shoulders and then one around his own.

Nancy gasped as she took in the beautiful scene which lay out in front of her. The snow reflected the hotel's lights and the glow from the moon. As she exhaled her breath fogged thickly in front of her, obscuring the eerie yellow-silverness of the ether.

"This is..." Nancy was speechless.

"Yes, it is," replied Torben.

Everything was still apart from the falling snow, which made the view seem unreal and magical. The undulating hills loomed in the background, the little chapel completely obscured from view.

Torben gestured to the landscape and said, "So tell me about your daring expedition."

Nancy tutted and rolled her eyes. "I just went for a little hike to explore the chapel, it looked so pretty from down here. Plus, I didn't want to stay cooped up in the hotel the whole time, I wanted to get out in this beautiful scenery. I was only gone a couple of hours and then the wives scooped me up and... well you know the rest."

"Tessa was so worried she was beside herself."

"Well, that was a massive over-reaction. But I'm sorry I worried her."

"She had us all lined up and ready to come and find you."

"You would have come and searched for me?"

Torben nodded, then opened his mouth as if to say something but closed it again quickly. The wind changed direction and thick freezing flakes started darting into their faces, forcing them to squint against the aggressive deluge.

"Mets mo mack minside!" Nancy said, her mouth filling with snow.

Torben opened the door and bundled her back into the warm. In their rush to get inside Nancy slipped and skidded, ending

44

up in a heap on the dark floor. She felt herself being helped back to her feet by a strong hand.

"Didn't spill a drop," she announced, raising her mug and laughing.

"That's quite a talent you've got there." Torben kept hold of Nancy for maybe a second longer than he needed to. "Let's get downstairs and warm up." His accent sounded thicker than normal, as if all his energy was going towards something else.

Bursting back through the 'staff only' door, they were spotted immediately by Catherine.

"Come and join us," she cooed, "we're just about to play Scrabble."

Nancy looked at Torben and rapidly tried to think of a reason to not go, she wanted to spend more time getting to know him. A chant of "Nancy! Nancy! Nancy!" started rumbling from the other players.

To her surprise Torben said, "Why not?" And then more quietly so that only Nancy could hear, he said, "They want to hear about your brave bjerg adventure." He nudged her as he gently teased her.

Nancy elbowed him back and muttered, "Don't complain when we get stuck playing games- this is your fault!"

***

Torben insisted on seeing Nancy back safely to her room. "They might want to send out a search party again if I don't know you've made it safely," he said and laughed.

"So, this is me," Nancy said shyly, turning to Torben, her back to her doorway.

"Nancy," Torben hesitated, "will..."

"Yes?"

Somehow Torben had found Nancy's hand and was holding it, stroking it with his thumb. Nancy's head felt light from laughing all evening, and possibly a bit from the rum. She tried to remember if she had left the room tidy, anticipating what Torben was going to ask.

"Nancy, will you come away with me?"

"Oh, I... I don't know what to say."

Torben dropped her hand and said gruffly, "I've put you in an uncomfortable position, I shouldn't have said anything."

"No, it's not that at all, I just wasn't expecting you to say that." Nancy laughed awkwardly. "I'd love to but when? Where? What about Tessa?"

His face lit up as he said, "Tessa could come too, and Neil. You can all come to my cabin for the weekend."

"That sounds wonderful."

"We can discuss it more tomorrow, good night."

Nancy felt for the door handle and with her other hand gave a small, self-conscious wave as she backed through the door. "Good night."

As Torben walked back to his own room, he felt elated- she'd said she'd love to go away with him! Suddenly, his mood darkened, what if she didn't feel the same way as him though? What if she was just the same as his ex. He shook his head as if to rid it of negative thoughts; he knew that Nancy was different. He firmly told himself to be more upbeat, it wouldn't be hard- he already felt like he was walking on air.

Chapter six.

"I can't believe that you've already agreed, without even asking me," moaned Tessa.

"I thought it was a lovely offer, why would I say no?"

"Eurgh, you know I've always hated stuff like this."

"We'll get a chance to spend some proper time together and Neil's invited too, if you want?" replied Nancy, who couldn't understand Tessa's negativity.

"That's not the point. Plus... it's Torben..."

"What's wrong with Torben?"

Tessa huffed and said, "He's sooooo, ugh...he's so Torben."

"If it's bothering you that much I can say no to him. I just thought it was a nice idea."

"Yeah, you should say no. Tell him that we've already made other plans..."

Before Nancy could reply, the women were interrupted with a cheery greeting from Neil. "Heeeeeey! Cabin buddies!" he called out as he grasped Tessa around one shoulder and offered up a closed fist to Nancy.

Nancy looked sideways at Neil, but he kept his hand there and looked expectantly at her.

She made a fist and bumped it into his as she said, "So, we're fist bumpers now, are we?"

Neil laughed and said, "Well, we *are* gonna be sharing a cabin in the woods. I thought it could be our thing."

Nancy nodded to the side as she shrugged and said, "Seeing as you put it like that..." Nancy stuck her fist out and said, "Cabin buddies!"

Neil grinned and banged knuckles again.

"What are you talking about?" asked Tessa.

"I just saw Torben, he told me we're all going to his cabin this weekend. It's gonna be epic, a real Danish cabin... in the woods. I can't wait!"

Nancy tried to keep a straight face as she watched Tessa realise that there was really no way out of it.

Unable to resist tormenting her just a bit, Nancy stuck her fist out towards Tessa and said, "Cabin buddies?!"

Tessa raised her eyebrows and through gritted teeth replied, "Cabin buddies."

At that moment, Catherine came into the lobby and said, "Ah, just the people I wanted to see. Come on, it's time for the farewell breakfast. George wants everyone there before he begins his 'thank you' speech. It's the last day of the conference today, so there's a lot to get through."

Tessa stood up straighter at the sight of her and replied, "We're just coming Mrs Lang." But Catherine was already walking off, looking for other stragglers.

When she had gone, Nancy looked to Tessa and Neil with a puzzled expression and said, "Why is George doing a farewell speech?"

Tessa tutted as Neil said, "Mr Lang? He's the boss. Didn't you know?"

"Is he? Crikey, you'd never know from talking with him."

"Really, Nancy, you've been hanging around with them the whole time. How did you not know?" said Tessa.

"You never said! Oh gosh, the boss...and his wife... I hope I haven't done anything embarrassing."

"Me too!" replied Tessa and laughed.

Tessa linked one arm through Nancy's and grabbed hold of Neil's hand. The three of them made their way through to the dining room.

The smell of bacon and coffee filled the air. Nancy's stomach gave a rumble which was luckily covered by the lively babble in the room. Once all the seats had been filled George stood up, drawing immediate silence and attention.

"Well, I won't keep you long. I'd just like to say, it's been another fantastic conference for Danglish...." George paused as he allowed a ripple of a cheer go around. "Thank you for all your hard work. I started Danglish twenty years ago with my Danish cousin, Anders. Although it's been 4 years since we lost him..." George wiped a tear from his eye. "...we still carry on with his vision to bring together our two wonderful cultures." There was more applause while George composed himself. "Danglish is at the forefront of its field, brokering relationships between UK and Danish businesses and sharing not only our expertise but our values and customs too."

A chorus of "Oooohhhhhh" went through Nancy's head as she listened. She smiled and thought- so *that's* what Danglish does.

"So, here's to us. To all of you faithful and dedicated employees who work so hard to keep our business the number one Anglo-Danish corporation, and to all of you here who support us." George nodded and smiled at his wife. "It's been a thought-provoking week and I've had some interesting insights from people that have been working with me since the company's inception," George gestured to some colleagues before catching Nancy's eye and saying, "and from some new faces too."

Nancy felt her cheeks colour at the

unexpected attention and missed the rest of his speech as she tried to remember anything incriminating that she might have said. She raised her glass with the rest of the group and said, "To Danglish!" as the speech ended.

Chapter seven.

The conference had finished early on its final day, allowing the group to make their way to the cabin while it was still daylight. They wound their way through endless farmland, bleak in the January light. The road petered out into a track as they bumped up and down it into the depths of a forest.

"We're here," announced Torben as he killed the engine.

"Yay!" called out Nancy as she unclipped her seatbelt.

Neil had already jumped out to start unloading and once Nancy was out of the car he insisted on another fist bump.

"Cabin buddies!" laughed Nancy, high with the excitement of their weekend getaway into the woods.

The temperature was in minus figures and although it was dry, the cold nipped at every part of her that was exposed. Nancy's case felt rather light as she was wearing virtually everything that she had brought with her. She carried it in to the small cabin and dumped it just inside the entrance before heading back to unload some more.

Out of the boot, Nancy wrestled one of the paper bags which was filled with supplies for their little trip away and lugged that up to the cabin door too. Strong arms relieved her of the heavy load.

"Thanks Neil," said Nancy gratefully. "Where's Tessa gone?"

"I've not seen her, maybe she's still unloading?"

At that moment, Torben strode into the cabin bearing another bulging paper bag. "That's the last of it," he said, as he shut the door with his foot.

"Is Tessa not still out there?" Nancy's voice had notes of both confusion and worry in.

"No, she said she was coming in to warm up."

"Where on earth is she then?" said Nancy as she looked around the cabin properly for the first time.

In the middle of the back wall was a large fire place, flanked by iron pokers. Strung brightly across the breast were some pretty, red and white, woven paper hearts. An old thick rug lay out in front of the hearth, echoing the colour scheme. A couple of mismatched sofas surrounded it, looking comfy and appealing.

Torben headed over to the small kitchenette. The red gingham table cloth on the dining table was barely visible under all the bags lumped on top and Torben started to put away the shopping while Nancy and Neil gazed around the cabin. He was determined to put aside his petty differences with Tessa for Nancy's sake. He resolved to try and get on with Tessa and consider her annoying immaturity as fun playfulness; she was Nancy's best friend after all.

"Perhaps she went to choose a bedroom?" said Torben, indicating to the dark doorway on the other side of the room.

Nancy headed over to it and called out, "Tessa?"

She heard a grunting sound in response and looked at the two men in consternation.

"Here, take this torch," said Torben, "while I sort out the power."

Although it was not too late in the afternoon, it was already getting darker outside and the cabin was gloomy. Nancy took the torch gratefully.

The bright light of the beam revealed wooden panelling on the walls as Nancy peered along the corridor. She turned into the first doorway she came to. The bathroom was simple but practical, with a deep looking bath and a pile of fluffy towels. Tessa was not in here.

Nancy shone the torch into the next room, which she found to be a bedroom. There was a lump under the bed sheets with an odd light emanating from underneath. Tutting, Nancy pulled back the covers.

"Tessa, what are you doing under here?"

Tessa was clutching her phone. Scowling, she looked up at her and grabbed for the covers. "It's frreeeeezzing!" she moaned.

"We can soon get it all toasty once we light a fire. Come on, you're being antisocial."

"I'm not moving from here, it's too cold. And I have no phone signal. This place is the pits."

"Of course you don't have any signal, we're in the middle of the woods. Come onnnnnn, you can't stay in here. Let's go and help the guys get the power sorted. You never know, maybe there'll be internet once the power's running."

Tessa pulled the top throw off the bed and wrapped it round herself like a shawl. She reluctantly followed behind Nancy, back out to join the others.

"I see you've chosen your room," said Torben.

"Yeah, it'll do I suppose," said Tessa, rather unkindly.

"Tessa, this is Torben's cabin; he should call the shots," said Nancy. Two small lines creased on her forehead and she felt like a kindergarten teacher.

Torben just smiled and said, "It

doesn't matter, I want you all to feel welcome."

Nancy smiled at him sincerely.

"So, shall I take the bags through to the rooms?" said Neil.

"Yes please. The girls can be in the nearest one, it's warmer, and we'll take the back room,' replied Torben.

Nancy was surprised he'd split the sleeping arrangements into girls and boys, but decided it was for the best. Now she wouldn't spend ages agonising over how to ask who was sleeping where. Tessa looked thunderous at the prospect of not sharing with Neil and sat down on one of the sofas with a huff.

Torben was squatting in front of the fire, stacking a careful pyramid of firelighters and kindling. The small pile of wood stacked next to the hearth was rapidly diminishing.

"Anything I can do to help?" asked Nancy.

Torben turned and looked at Tessa and then up at Nancy. "We'll need to go and get more firewood while there's still some light. Don't get anything too heavy, I'll do that, but if you could find some more kindling, I'd appreciate that."

"No problem. Come on Tessa, let's go and forage for some kindling."

"I'm not going outside, I'll catch my death."

Nancy's shoulders tensed but she was determined not to let her frustration with Tessa get the better of her. "The activity will warm you up, plus we need the wood to make the fire so...chop chop."

Neil walked back in at that moment and spotting the unintended pun, laughed loudly. "Chop chop...good one Nancy! Right, I'll go and get some wood too then."

Seeing Neil heading for the door was enough to rouse Tessa from the sofa and the trio went outside. Tessa followed Neil closely and they walked round to a log pile at the side of the building.

The snow was an eerie muffler to any sounds and the cabin stood, grey and lonely in the forest. There was just a faint orange glow coming through a small window. Grabbing a dusty old basket and some tools from the porch Nancy headed off to pick up old branches and small bits of wood that would dry quickly.

Under the thick canopy of a large tree she found some sticks that hadn't been covered in snow. Kneeling down, she filled her basket with suitable kindling. Standing up, she stretched and then brushed the old pine needles off her knees. She noticed a holly bush, the blood red berries glistening like jewels against the snowy back drop. She snipped off some sprigs and held them like a prickly bouquet. Then she found some soft evergreen fronds, bluey-green, to add to the arrangement. It was getting too difficult to see the foliage so she decided she had enough for a pretty display.

Laden down, she turned back towards the cabin and an entirely different scene greeted her. Darkness had swallowed them quickly and the lodge shone out like a welcoming star in the black night. Candles were lit in each little window and a strong, bright light flickered out from the front door. The smell of pine and wood-smoke in the air and the tell-tale stream of silver curling out of the chimney showed that Torben had got the fire going.

"The place looks amazing from outside!" called out Nancy as she banged the snow off her boots and bundled herself through the door.

"Thank you for getting all that. Put the kindling over there, by the big cabinet in the corner," said Torben. He was busy in the kitchen area.

Tessa was perched in her previous spot in front of the fire, but this time with a smile on her face and a steaming mug in her hand. Neil was rubbing her feet. As she looked around the room, Nancy could see it was transformed with the magical dancing light from almost a hundred candles. Every single surface was crammed with them. She swept her eyes around and they finally came to rest on Torben, who was looking sombre.

As he passed her a steaming mug of something he said, "I'm so sorry, we have no power. The generator's broken."

"Who needs a generator when there's all this," exclaimed Nancy as she raised a hand, gesturing to the whole room.

Relief flooded Torben's face. "You don't mind? It won't be everyone's idea of fun." He looked pointedly in the direction of Tessa and pulled a face.

"Of course I don't mind," said Nancy. Then she took a swig from her mug and said, "Mmmmm, thanks."

The drink was sweet and hot with a strong apple flavour, there was an after burn of something alcoholic which Nancy considered to be not at all unpleasant. As she took a couple more sips it warmed her all the way down to her toes.

Overhearing the conversation, Tessa sat bolt upright as she realised the implications. "How are we going to cook dinner if there's no power?" she asked, the smile quickly slipping from her face.

Torben grinned at her, his face transforming with his cheeky, boyish smile. "We'll cope, you'll see," he replied mysteriously. He was determined not to let Tessa's moaning get to him.

"Have you got a vase? I'd brought in some cuttings to brighten the place up, but... it doesn't really need brightening now," said Nancy sheepishly.

"It was a nice thought though," replied Torben. He easily reached a vase down from the top of the tall wooden cabinet and passed it to her.

Nancy filled it with water then plunged in the bunch of holly and evergreen and placed it in the middle of the table.

"Very festive," said Torben. With the glow of the flames, the scent of pine, and Nancy's wonderful company, he really did feel very festive.

Chapter eight.

The little group of four sat huddled around the cheery fire. A pot was suspended over it and the rich smell of simmering tomatoes and herbs filled the air. They each had a poker with a chunk of bread spiked at the end and they held them in the flames, gently turning them round.

Before Nancy's was blackened too much, she took it out of the flames and cautiously prized it off the hot poker and on to a plate. Giving it a moment to cool she then dipped the toast into a bowl of soup and took a big bite.

"Mmmmm," said Nancy as she savoured the flavours.

"It tastes better when you've made it yourself," commented Neil.

"I could murder a steak right now," said Tessa.

Nancy thought to herself, *I'll murder you in a minute if you don't stop moaning.* However, endeavouring to keep her cool she just smiled over to Torben and said, "Thanks for organising all this."

Torben smiled warmly back at her and said, "You're welcome." Then he added,

"Tessa, maybe you can come hunting with me tomorrow and see if we can catch you that steak?"

Tessa visibly blanched and everyone chuckled.

While sitting around the fire swapping stories Nancy felt prickles of excitement that reminded her of when she went camping or on an adventure in the forest when she was a child. She couldn't stop the small smile spreading across her face at the thought of those happy memories.

Torben had dug out an old trunk full of knitted jumpers, thick woollen socks and cosy slippers. Tessa and Neil had donned several extra layers to keep warm. Sitting snuggled in front of the roaring hearth, they looked like a couple of models from an eighties ski wear catalogue. Nancy had selected a grey, red and white poncho and some very woolly slippers with a pom-pom on top of each foot, which Torben referred to as 'house shoes'.

Noticing he had only selected some well-worn, orange house shoes from the trunk, Nancy asked, "Aren't you cold Torben?"

"No, I don't feel the cold. My family and I have been coming here all my life. This cabin has been owned by the Christensen's for generations. I've had many adventures in this forest."

"I'd love to hear about them," said

Nancy.

Tessa quickly interrupted and said, "I think I'm going to head off to bed now," and faked a yawn.

"I think I'd better hit the hay too," said Neil and they both scuttled off quickly.

"Was it something I said?" asked Torben.

Nancy laughed. "No, it's not you... it's definitely Tessa," she said with a sigh. "Sorry she's so... rude, she's not usually like this. I'm not sure what's got into her."

It was Torben's turn to laugh. "I've worked with Tessa long enough to know that she likes the finer things in life and that she's a city girl at heart. Don't worry about it."

She rolled her eyes and then said, "That's a very polite way of saying she's being a complete diva. Let's get some more to drink and you can tell me more about your adventures here."

Nancy stacked some extra logs on the fire while Torben made some more drinks. With full mugs in hand, they snuggled up on the sofa. Nancy tucked her pom-pommed feet under Torben's thigh to keep them extra cosy and he spread a thick blanket over the top of them.

"You go first," he said. "Tell me about your childhood in the woods then I'll tell you mine."

"How did you know I spent my

childhood in the woods."

"I told you, I know a kindred spirit when I see one."

Snow started to fall outside again but this served only to make the cabin feel safer and cosier; like they were cocooned in a chrysalis. The couple nestled together and stayed up talking like this for hours.

***

Neil pulled a woolly jumper off, revealing a toned chest underneath as all the other layers rose up.

"Brrrr," he said, as he pulled the clothing back down. "Let's get into bed and warm up!"

Tessa had already climbed in, fully clothed, and wrapped the duvet over her head again, only her face and a lock of her raven hair showing.

"It's soooooo cold," she moaned.

"It'll be ok, it's just like camping. We have to generate our own heat," he raised one eyebrow seductively as he climbed under the bedcover and pulled Tessa towards him.

"Do you really not hate this?" Tessa asked.

Neil briefly wondered why Tessa wasn't happy; they were on a fun break away with her best friend.

"What's to hate? We are in a cabin... in the forest! Torben's taking me hunting tomorrow... this is the best weekend ever."

Tessa had started creeping her fingers under his top to find the muscly torso she had just caught a glimpse of but she stopped suddenly and looked at him with an 'I'm not amused' expression on her face.

"Oh, and did I not mention... I have the pleasure of a beautiful, clever and funny woman's company."

"Ok, I get why you don't hate this now."

Tessa carried on roaming her hand over his smooth body and all other thoughts left Neil's head. He kissed her hungrily on the mouth as she wrapped a leg around him and pulled him in, even closer to her.

***

Nancy awoke to the first shafts of grey light creeping in to the room and saw the red embers in the grate from the dying fire. The woollen blanket itched her face, but as she went to move it away she found that one of her hands was curled tightly into one of Torben's. Not wanting to wake him, Nancy carefully prised her hand from his and wriggled out from the knot of limbs and blankets.

Thankful for the house shoes she was still wearing, she straightened the poncho on her shoulders and tended to the fire. Restacking it with kindling and some smaller logs to get it going again. The wood pile was quickly shrinking.

As she bent down to clear up the dirty mugs which were dotted over the rug, she caught sight of Torben's face in the dim light. He was sleeping soundly, his profile looked youthful and happy as he rested, and Nancy wondered where the morose grumpy character that she met at the airport had come from. While she was looking at him, he suddenly opened his eyes and saw her standing over him.

"I didn't mean to startle you."

"You didn't," said Torben, his face creased into a smile. "You're a lovely sight to wake up to."

Scanning down over her random knitted ensemble Nancy grimaced and said, "I think I've looked better."

"I think you look very hyggelig."

"Huggable?" questioned Nancy, mishearing the Danish word. "Are you trying to tell me I look fat?" She withdrew slightly from standing near him and placed her hands on her hips.

"No!" said Torben chuckling. "Hyggelig. It's a compliment." He reached up and grabbed at her hands pulling her down on to him.

"What does it mean?" Thoughts of glamour and beauty flew through Nancy's head as she tried to decipher the compliment, her heart rate quickening at her sudden proximity to him.

"It doesn't translate."

"It must," she said. Nancy turned and started tickling him, demanding, "Tell me!"

Eventually, he managed to choke out a couple words of explanation. "Cosy, I guess... safe... snuggly..."

Nancy stopped tickling and sat back from Torben, clearly disappointed. "Oh," she said.

"It is my most favourite thing," said Torben drawing her nearer to him and gently moving his hands up under the many knitted layers.

He pulled her in for a long kiss which warmed her far better than the fire that was heating up in the grate. Nancy moved her hands into his hair and tugged him closer to her. She could feel the slight scratch of stubble on her soft skin and the clinging smell of wood-smoke filled her nose. They were completely lost in the moment until the sound of the door clanking open rang out and startled them.

Nancy sprung up, adrenaline and a hint of guilt coursing through her. She looked over to the door and saw Tessa and Neil standing watching them, their hair was tousled and they had smirks on their faces.

"Sorry to disturb you," said Tessa.

"You didn't," replied Nancy, her voice slightly higher pitched than normal. "Shall I put the kettle on?"

"I'll heat up some water over the fire," said Torben, standing up.

"Sorry, Torben," said Neil. "Did you sleep out here because Tessa had come into our room? I just didn't think..."

"Ha ha, no problem," replied Torben. "I didn't even make it that far. We fell asleep chatting."

"It must have been riveting," said Tessa snarkily and Nancy shot her a scowl. She was starting to get a bit wound up by Tessa's constant griping.

Chapter nine.

"Find us something tasty for dinner," said Nancy, as she pressed a thermos of hot soup into Torben's hands.

"Yeah, good luck doing the hunter-gatherer thing. We'll stay here keeping the cabin warm." Tessa sounded like she had no intention of doing anything helpful.

"I'm pretty sure, in the old days, men and women shared the hunter-gatherer *thing*," said Neil. He raised an eyebrow at Tessa but was clearly not really annoyed with her laziness.

Torben laughed and said, "I'm sure the ladies will appreciate whatever we manage to bring back for them." He bent forward and gave Nancy a tender kiss on each cheek before striding outside.

Neil insisted on fist bumping with Nancy and then gave Tessa a passionate, back-bending kiss before following. Nancy smiled as she watched the men trudge across the snow and disappear amongst the trees. Her face soon dropped as she caught sight of Tessa's smirk.

"What?" Nancy asked her, readjusting her poncho.

"It's just funny."

"What's funny?"

"I get sexy Neil and you're stuck with Torben the Tiresome."

"What do you mean stuck? I like Torben, what's your problem with him?"

"He's just sooooo dull," said Tessa.

Nancy wanted to grab her friend and scream *why are you being such a bitch?* But she didn't. She took a deep breath and counted to ten as she slowly exhaled. Then she changed the subject. The last thing she needed was a showdown.

"What shall we do with our free time? Do you fancy sitting on the porch with some hot chocolate and having a chat?"

"Nah, I might have a dip in the bath," said Tessa and then sauntered off.

"But we've not had chance to catch up yet," said Nancy quietly. Tessa didn't reply. Feeling hurt, Nancy turned back to the sink and winced in the freezing water as she rinsed her hands. "Tessa..." she started to warn her.

"What?" shouted Tessa from the bedroom. Her voice was full of irritation.

"Nothing," said Nancy, equally irritated. "She can find out for herself," she muttered under her breath.

Nancy crossed to the fire and stoked some more logs onto it. The yellow and orange flames licked over the wood and whistled out some sparks. Surveying the rapidly diminishing wood pile, she realised some more foraging for kindling was in order.

She called out to Tessa, "I'm gonna go and get some more wood." But there was no reply.

***

"Let's head this way to start with," suggested Torben.

"Is there good hunting this way?"

"I'm hoping we can do some good 'gathering'," said Torben, mysteriously.

Torben led them along the bank of a river to a slippery, icy bridge. The quickly moving water rushing beneath them.

"So, things seem to be going well between you and Nancy," called out Neil as they shuffled over it, single file.

Torben stopped half way across and turned to him. "Yes. I like her a lot."

Surprised by the sudden intensity on Torben's face, he nodded not sure of what to say; it seemed that he wanted to open up.

Torben turned to face the oncoming water and rested his forearms on the edge of the bridge, Neil mirrored his posture. Torben seemed to be working up to saying something. He paused for a while and then continued, "She's even stopped me being such a grumpy old man."

"I never thought you were..."

Torben held up a finger and chuckled. "I'm sure everyone at work thinks I'm grumpy *and* boring... I *wanted* to be grumpy and boring... I got rather good at it. I haven't been on a date for four years."

Neil didn't say anything, letting Torben take his time. Staring straight ahead he said, "My last girlfriend... she... she put me off women for a while."

The men stood together, staring out, while the gushing water filled the silence. Suddenly Torben straightened up and said, "But it's a bad habit, being so morose all the time, I'm working on breaking it." Without saying anything else he turned and continued to traverse the bridge.

As they carried on walking Neil shook his head in disbelief and, under his breath, repeated, "Four years?!"

"This is our neighbour's house," said Torben, as they approached a similar wooden cabin, standing alone and empty.

Neil hesitated as Torben mounted the steps up to the porch. "Are we allowed up here?"

"They won't mind," he said smiling. He reached up to the top of the door frame and pulled down a key.

***

Absorbed in her work, Nancy wasn't aware of the shrieking until Tessa had come fully outside. She was wearing nothing but a towel.

"There's. No. Hot. Water!"

Nancy looked over from her spot, kneeling under a tree. "Oh gosh, she's gone mad," she said to herself. Then she called out, "There's no power, so I guess not."

"But I'm frrreeeeezzzing!" squealed Tessa.

"Go and put some clothes on then."

There was a guttural roar from Tessa and she turned on her heel and went back inside. Sensing that Tessa needed some TLC, Nancy waded through the snow and back up the porch steps. She kicked her shoes off and put the wood on the pile with the rest of the kindling.

"Tessa," she called out softly as she knocked on their bedroom door, not that either of them had slept in it yet.

She turned the knob and slowly went into the room. Tessa was just pulling Nancy's winter jumper over her head.

"I can't believe you brought me to this hell hole."

"So, you found my *ugly* sweater then," said Nancy, by way of reply. Any inclination to soothe Tessa had evaporated with Tessa's fiery outburst.

"Lending me this is the least you can do. I don't think I've ever been so cold in my life."

Determined to keep calm, Nancy fought her urge to argue back. "I know it's chilly," she said patiently, "but you'll warm up a bit if you get moving; get your blood flowing."

"I'll warm up when we finally leave."

Seeing she wouldn't get anything civil out of Tessa, Nancy took another calming breath and said, "I'm getting some more wood. You're welcome to come and join me." Then she turned and marched out.

It had started snowing again and the flakes mixed with her tears as she let her emotions finally overflow. Nancy felt so isolated. She was alone in the middle of a snow storm, in the middle of a forest, in the middle of a foreign country...in the middle of a crisis. She really needed her friend and her friend was being a selfish bitch. She stood on the porch and allowed herself to cry for two whole minutes. Then hastily wiping her eyes on her cuffs, she sniffed loudly and went to find the axe.

"Someone needs to do something around here," she huffed to herself.

***

The men trudged through the freezing landscape until suddenly Torben braced his arm against Neil, stopping him from stepping any further. He put his finger to his lips and then pointed to some fresh tracks in the snow. Torben led Neil carefully forwards, quietly and slowly, following the imprints.

Around them, the pine trees started to thin and they found themselves on the edge of a clearing. The tracks went on but the men stayed right on the periphery; camouflaged in the trees. Following the direction with their eyes, the men froze. With a thick, shaggy winter coat and the sun glancing off its tremendous antlers, the men watched the huge creature walk hesitantly across the open space.

"Is that a... a stag?" asked Neil, agape.

"Yes, a male red deer. I'd say about 7 years old."

The men watched the glorious creature paw at the snow, revealing something tasty underneath.

"We're not going to hunt it, are we?"

Torben let out a chuckle, startling the deer which looked over to them and then dashed off, quickly swallowed by the trees across the clearing.

"No. Sorry, I think I scared it off."

"Phew! That's such a magnificent beast, I don't think I could..."

"We'd never finish it all," replied Torben. "And besides, I brought out tins of provisions, so we don't *actually* need to hunt."

"But you said to Tessa and Nancy that we were hunting." Neil sounded confused.

"Nah, we can still track the animals though. I thought it would be nice to give them some time alone together."

"Good idea. I sensed Tessa was getting annoyed that she couldn't have a good chat with Nancy."

"Hmmmm," said Torben, a frown furrowed his brow. "I think Nancy was getting frustrated that she hadn't managed to see much of Tessa. This'll be a good chance for them to work it out, surely?"

"I hope so. Leaving them alone together- in the woods- what can possibly go wrong?"

Both of them looked at each other and Neil pretended to grimace.

Chapter ten.

Thwack, thwack, thwack. After a couple of attempts, Nancy was getting the hang of chopping the wood. She had found a stump with the axe embedded in it at the side of the cabin. There were plenty of logs already there to chop up and Nancy was getting stuck in; splitting bigger ones into smaller chunks and then tossing them into a wicker basket. The physical exertion was cathartic. The snow was still gently falling and Nancy welcomed the cooling kisses on her cheeks as she worked up a sweat.

"Nancy..." a plaintive cry rung out from the front door.

"What?" she shouted back, annoyed to be brought back to reality.

"Something's happened to the fire," shouted Tessa.

"Put another log on it," she called back, frustration straining her voice.

"I did, it didn't work. I think it's gone out."

Nancy cast the axe down with such force that the blade stuck into the stump. She tossed the last couple of logs in to the basket and hauled it up into her arms.

Staggering slightly under the weight, the power of irritation kept her steady and she made her way back around the cabin. The falling snow had filled in her tracks and she could barely make out the steps up the porch, a thick white blanket had blown in, covering everywhere.

She spied Tessa hovering in the doorway, she had clearly no intention of coming outside and Nancy's irritation peaked. Juggling the cumbersome load and guessing at her footwork, she made her way up the steps; clunking up one at a time. As her feet finally made their way on to the porch, Nancy's arms began to tremble with the strain. Not wanting to drop her cargo, she rushed forward towards the open doorway. Her foot slipped on the icy wood, forcing her into front splits. The basket thunked down loudly next to her.

Tessa giggled. She couldn't help herself. Her friend was dressed in about eight layers of clothing, her curly hair was covered in snow and wood splinters; she looked like a mad forest lady. As she watched her approach, she was eye-level one second and then had suddenly disappeared, dropping about four feet downwards, into the most incredible gymnastic feat.

"Whoops!" said Tessa, chuckling.

"Whoops?" said Nancy, no longer containing the anger in her voice.

"Whoops?"

Tessa laughed again but this time slightly nervously.

"You could at least come and help me."

Tessa pulled on her snow boots and reluctantly came out onto the porch, shuddering in the cold air. She stuck out her hand and helped pull Nancy on to her feet. A giggle escaped Tessa's lips again and Nancy glared. Nancy bent forwards and grabbed a hold of both handles. As she lifted the basket of wood up the bottom split and the wood promptly tumbled down onto the snow-covered planks. Tessa chuckled again. Huffing, Nancy bent down to collect up the wood but at the last moment changed her mind, instead, her hands closed around a pile of snow. She scooped it upwards and threw it over Tessa.

"Brrrr-urgh!" Tessa yelled. "What was that for?"

"Thought it might give you something to laugh about," said Nancy as she bent back down for more of the white stuff.

This time she patted the snow into an orange sized ball. She launched it at Tessa's torso, but her aim was slightly out and it hit her right in the forehead. It was Nancy's turn to chuckle nervously, as Tessa spluttered and wiped her face.

There was a moment's pause and then Tessa dropped to the ground and rapidly started to form several snowballs. Nancy ran down the steps, scooping snow off the hand rail as she went. They both aimed for each other simultaneously and snow exploded into the air. Tessa followed with two more, one finding its mark right on Nancy's backside as she ran away.

Nancy used the wood pile as a makeshift shelter and began to arm herself, forming more snowballs as she waited for Tessa to come around and find her. The ball came whizzing at Nancy before she had time to react. Tessa was coming around the side of the house with an onslaught of icy weapons.

As one clocked Nancy on her arm, Tessa called out, "That's for getting snow in my ear."

Nancy fired back and shouted, "Well, that's for laughing at me."

"That's for bringing me to this hell hole." The snow clipped Nancy's shoulder. Tessa flung another snowball and shouted, "It's worse than that, at least hell would be *warm*."

Nancy ducked behind her shelter and made some more snowballs. Despite the melting ice trickling down her back she was fired up and ready to battle.

"That's for being such a moaning *bitch*," Nancy shrieked. She jumped up and fired at Tessa. Her missile smacked her opponent in the chest.

"Ouch! That's. For. Hitting. Me. In. The. Boob." Each word was punctuated by Tessa throwing another snowball.

Nancy threw two, one from each hand. "These are for being lazy and buggering off with Neil the whole time."

"Me buggering off? What about you and Torben?" Tessa stood with her hands on her hips, affronted by Nancy's accusation. Another snowball hit its target. "Urgh!" she grunted and launched one back.

"This is for being rude to poor Torben."

"You deserve it, he's the most boring man I've ever met. He's kiss-you-on-the-cheek-bore-you-to-tears dull!"

"No he's not! He's a gentleman. And I happen to find him interesting."

"That's 'cos you've turned boring too!" Tessa aimed another snowball with her hateful comment. "You wouldn't come out with me and Neil, I tried to include you but noooo you were too busy with Tooooorrrr-ben."

"You'd already ditched me for Neil by then," yelled Nancy. She frantically sculpted some more snowy weapons. "This is for talking 'shop' with Neil, the whole time."

"This is for you not saying ANYTHING!"

With a scream the girls quit throwing

balls at each other, instead flinging armfuls of loose snow over each other. Bending and scooping and throwing in a frenzy.

Thunk. Thunk. Two snowballs struck them each on the leg with quite a force. They stopped and looked into the forest. On the edge of the trees stood Torben and Neil, both with an armful of ready-made balls.

"Eeek!" The girls looked at each other, then dived behind the wood pile.

They peeked over the top but two more balls came whistling past, missing them by centimetres. They started to scoop together more snow, getting into a system with Tessa making the balls and Nancy launching them.

Surveying the situation, Nancy said, "They're only throwing balls at us when we pop up to throw some at them."

Tessa popped her head up to look and again another ball came sailing quickly past. "You're right. And it doesn't look like they've moved position."

"What are we going to do? We're stuck here, but I think they're stuck there too."

"Let's wait them out."

"Are you sure it's not too cold for you?" asked Nancy, a very slight hint of bitterness to her voice.

"No, I've got all warmed up since we've been having the snowball fight," Tessa replied, sounding sheepish.

Nancy gave her a steady look and

then broke into a smile. Tessa smiled too, relief flooding her face and reached over to give her best friend a hug.

"I'm so sorry. I've been a selfish bitch."

"Yes, but I've not been perfect either," replied Nancy.

"I was so excited that you were coming to visit, there's so much I wanted to do with you and then, when I got together with Neil, it was like everything was going perfectly. But then, I felt like you weren't excited for me and didn't want to do stuff and you wouldn't talk to me, I... I felt like you were holding something back from me. And that hurt so... I acted like a complete bitch." Tessa looked up into Nancy's eyes, guilty and breathless from her confession.

"I *was* holding something back," admitted Nancy. "It wasn't that I wasn't excited for you and happy to see you. I just really needed to see you for me, for my own benefit and there I found you, with everything going so right for you, and with everything going so wrong for me. Well, it was hard to swallow. I could never find the right moment and I just couldn't bring myself to tell you."

"Tell me what?"

Nancy took a deep breath and then said, "I've lost my job."

"What? Your PA job?"

"Yeah, I'm not on annual leave from

work right now. I don't actually have a job to take annual leave from. The company's folding and I've been made redundant." A single tear fell onto her cheek.

Tessa embraced her friend, burrowing her head into her neck and squeezing her tight for as long as she needed.

"It feels better to say it out loud," said Nancy with a forced laugh. "And, I know, it could be worse, but still... it's just so unexpected. I have no idea what to do."

"We'll think of something together," said Tessa and squeezed her hand reassuringly. "I really want that hot chocolate on the porch now."

"Me too. It feels good to talk...but I guess we could be warmer. Let's make a run for it," said Nancy.

"Let's do this." Tessa made a fist and offered it to Nancy. "Cabin buddies?" she said hopefully.

"Cabin buddies!" said Nancy as she laughed.

They gathered up the rest of their ammunition and then staying crouched down, darted out from behind their shelter, throwing snowballs in the general direction of their assailants.

Fire was immediately returned and the men, who had waited for the girls to make a move, came out from their spot behind the trees and started running towards them. They could hear the guys laughing as they came steadily closer. Snow bursting as it landed around them.

It was no use, Torben and Neil were about to overpower them. They were getting nearer and nearer.

"Run!" shouted Tessa.

They threw their last remaining snowballs and sprinted with all their might. The snow drift slowed them down and soon Torben caught up with Nancy and Neil with Tessa. They tackled them both down to the ground.

Torben allowed Nancy just enough slack to roll onto her back, but pinned her down all the same. His weight overpowered her struggles and she looked up to his handsome face, lit up with joy and laughter.

His stubble tickled her cheeks as he whispered in her ear, "Do you submit?"

"Never!" she replied, laughing.

"Well, there's only one thing for it." Torben plunged his lips onto Nancy's, smothering them as he kissed her hard and deep. His hands snaked behind her head pulling her up towards him, while his fingers tangled into the coils of her hair.

"Now that's a kiss," said Tessa. Neil had let her sit up but he was still straddling her.

Neil kissed Tessa on the nose and said, "Come on, let's go and get you thawed out."

Chapter eleven.

Flames were roaring in the grate again. Neil had stoked the fire and it was happily spitting and crackling away, giving the room a wholesome glow.

Torben let in an icy blast as he came through the door, shutting it quickly before bending over to take off his boots. Nancy gave his behind an appreciative glance as she sat snugly with Tessa. They'd taken off their cold, soaking clothes and changed into the remaining items in Torben's box of crazy knitwear. Now they were curled up under a blanket together, giggling.

"How much rum did you put in their hot chocolates?" asked Neil, watching them.

"Just enough," said Torben. "We don't want them to pass out, not now they're finally talking to each other."

"I guess the plan of yours worked," said Neil. "Well, at least they're friends again now."

"Yes, it was just a storm in a coffee pot."

"Teacup."

"Ah is that it? Or a storm in a snow globe perhaps?" He thumbed out of the window indicating to the swirling flurry continuing outside. "Although, if I knew that all it needed was a snowball fight, we could have saved ourselves the hike."

"But I wouldn't have got a tracking lesson, and we wouldn't have found the part to fix the generator."

"Indeed. I must get our neighbour a nice bottle of schnapps to thank him and to apologise for breaking into his cabin and taking one of his spares."

"I'm sure they'll appreciate that!" said Neil. He reached for their own half empty bottle of schnapps to pour some out for Torben and himself.

"Right, it's all sorted, shall I put the lights on now we have power?"

"No!" called out Tessa suddenly. They all turned to look at her. "What? I like the candles they're cosy."

Seeing everyone's bemused expression, Tessa pulled the bobble hat down over her face to hide. "Ooops, was I that bad?" she asked nervously, peeking out from underneath.

Torben chuckled benevolently while Neil tutted.

"Right, let's play a board game," said Neil as he walked over to the armoire.

"Anything but Scrabble!" shouted Torben and Nancy in unison. Catching each other's eye, they smirked.

"I'd feel like I was cheating on

Catherine Lang," said Nancy.

"Let's play Monopoly," said Tessa as she saw the familiar box amongst the giant stack of games at the top of the huge cupboard. "I'll be the banker."

"Is that because you don't need to be able to speak Danish to cheat at Danish Monopoly?" said Nancy and Tessa waggled her eyebrows in response.

Torben chuckled again before saying, "Ok, but I want to have the lucky boot."

***

"How have you won AGAIN?!" implored Tessa.

"You can't cheat a cheater," said Neil, knowingly as he fanned himself with all the colourful notes.

"This has been so much fun, it's taken me right back to when I was a boy here. Can I make a request?" said Torben.

"Yes, anything but another round of Monopoly," said Nancy, who'd gone bankrupt. Again. "This is all far too close to home."

Torben said, "There's still some light left, let's go tobogganing." Tessa started to interrupt but he held his hand up and carried on saying, "I'll make you my favourite dessert after, Æbletærte." He tried to persuade her to get back out in the snow.

"I was just gonna say, it sounds like a fab idea. I'm sorry I've been so grumpy everyone, I just hate being cold."

"Don't worry about it," replied Torben.

Neil leaned over and kissed Tessa's cheek and Nancy gave her a kind, forgiving smile.

"I'm wearing your coat though," Tessa said to Neil.

"I thought you might say that," he replied. Tessa bent towards him, giving him a cheeky grin and a peck on the lips.

"So, this dessert, it sounds like an apple tart?" said Nancy, hopefully.

"Yes, it's an apple pie but with a cinnamon crumble on top."

"Mmmmm, you had me at pie! Let's go," said Nancy.

While Tessa and Neil were bickering over jackets, Torben walked quietly over to the cabinet and opened its other door, inside hung some very thick wintery coats. He nodded his head towards them and said, "Feel free to help yourself to any of these."

"Wow," said Tessa as she jumped up and headed over to grope inside. "It looks like you could get to Narnia through there!"

Togged up in the Christensen family collection of warm jackets, the group made their way up the nearest slope. Torben and Neil dragged the two wooden sleds behind them. Listening hard, Nancy could only hear the whistle of the runners over the snow, the crunching of boots and the heavy breathing of the intrepid sledders as they climbed steadily upwards.

At the top, Nancy mounted the sled with an ungainly lunge. Her many layers of clothes and cumbersome boots made it difficult to stretch her leg wide to get it over the wooden slats. She was nervous that she would start sliding off unexpectedly. Torben expertly climbed on behind her and she felt his strong arm clutch around her waist. He drew her towards him. Butterflies flitted in her tummy and she wondered if he could feel them too, under all the layers. She recalled Torben saying he was feeling like a kid again, well so was she. She felt like a school girl besotted with her first love. Every look, every touch, set her alight. It didn't matter that it was cold out, even the thought of Torben was most definitely keeping her warm.

While waiting for Neil and Tessa to get set for the race, Torben nuzzled through Nancy's hair, inhaling the scent of her sweet perfume and nibbled her ear lobe.

"Mmmm," she couldn't help but groan slightly.

There was a volcano inside Torben, building up, ready to erupt. He couldn't hold himself back any longer, he'd been resisting for days, worried that it was far too soon.

"I think I'm falling in love with you, Nancy," he whispered, his breath hot on her cheek.

Before she could reply, Neil had shouted out "Go!" and Torben had kicked them off; racing against the other sled to see who could get to the bottom first. He gripped hold of the reins and he clung Nancy to him. The race was a symbol for everything he wanted; he wanted to protect her; he wanted to succeed for her. He had known since they met; he wanted her.

The wind whipped through her hair and stung her eyes. Trees flew by, a blur. With adrenaline rushing and her heart pounding with exhilaration, they zipped downwards. But it wasn't the thrill of the sleigh ride that had got her all worked up. Nancy was high; she was falling in love with someone and they felt the same. There was no better joy ride than that.

Chapter twelve.

A sheepish look passed over Tessa's face as Nancy tossed her the winter jumper.

"Are you sure I can borrow it?" asked Tessa.

"Yes! You don't normally stop to ask." Nancy pretended to be exasperated.

Tessa gave a nervous grin as she pulled it on over her head and then twirled slowly with her arms out to show it off. "How do I look?"

"Very winter chic. Why the change of heart? I thought you hated it when you saw me wear it."

"I massively underestimated how good it is to feel all warm and snuggly when it's so cold and snowy outside."

"Well, they do say that life's better in an ugly sweater."

"Do they?!" Tessa looked at Nancy like she had gone a bit mad.

"Well, I say that anyway," she replied with a grin and a cockily raised eyebrow.

Nancy sat down cross-legged on the bed while she waited for Tessa to finish getting ready.

"You've gone all quiet suddenly, are

you ok?" said Tessa.

"Sorry, I was in a world of my own."

"Are you thinking about your job?"

"Yeah, or lack of job, more like."

"Let's write a list of all the things you like doing and things that you're good at and see if we can come up with some inspiration."

"Ok, I'll have a think on this walk and we can brainstorm when we get back." Nancy seemed relieved to have a tentative plan and felt her shoulders relax down at least an inch.

Tessa nodded. "Sounds good to me and we'll get the boys to help too. Ok, I've layered up so let's gooooo!" She leapt from the room with a new-found enthusiasm.

The morning sun was bright in the blue sky, sparkling blindingly off the snow. The boughs of the trees were drooping heavily and occasionally shed their load, springing free and shaking the snow loose as it dripped and melted.

Nancy and Torben crunched along happily in front of Tessa and Neil as they headed off for a hike.

"It's not too far," said Torben. "There's a great alm on the edge of the forest, it has the best food. I've been going there for years."

"Are you warm enough?" Nancy turned back to ask Tessa.

"Well, I've got thick socks on, your

jumper, one of Torben's coats and a hot water bottle, so I think I'll be ok."

"Yeah, and if we keep the pace up that will help," said Neil.

"Yeah, I don't want to get crossty again."

"Crossty?" said Torben. "I don't know this English word."

"No one does," said Nancy with a laugh. "I think Tessa just made it up." Nancy looked enquiringly at her friend.

"It's a mash up. I get cross when I feel cold and frosty... crossty!"

The group laughed and then Neil said, "You get 'hangry' too."

Tessa's cheeks pinked up slightly and she said, "We'd better get moving then and get me to the amazing food."

Nancy entwined her hand into Torben's as they stomped along through the snow. He looked down into her green eyes, gazing intensely up at him.

"Everything ok?" said Torben.

"Yes. It's more than ok. I love this."

"I'm so glad you're enjoying it, and you seem such a natural here."

"What do you mean?"

"Well, you cycled around the city; you love the food..."

"And the drink!"

"You're just like me! You seem to love getting back to nature and then getting cosy and watching the snow storms. You love spending time with close friends, like they're your family."

"You're right, I do love all that. What was it you called me? Hoo-gah-like?" Lines gently creased Nancy's forehead as she pondered the phrase.

"Hyggelig."

"And 'hygge' means snuggly?"

"I told you it doesn't translate! But I guess the closest thing is being content with loved ones; enjoying the simple pleasures in life; being mindful."

"I see. I love hygge too!" said Nancy laughing. Then more seriously she said, "Thank you so much for making this weekend happen."

Torben leant over and kissed Nancy's head. "You are so very welcome," he said into her soft curls.

A smile rested on his face, which although had felt foreign to him a few days before, now felt exactly right. As they walked on, his heart felt light. He could see the light dancing on her sleek chestnut hair and her radiant smile shining brilliantly. He felt like he had been given a new lease of life, an opportunity to feel young again. He wondered if, perhaps, he felt better than his younger self, had he ever felt this happy before?

***

After two hours of wading through snow a welcoming wooden lodge came into view. There were benches and tables around the outside and the smell of wood-smoke entranced them as they got closer. Nancy and Tessa headed for the first table and sat down gratefully. Soft red rugs lined the seats and they wrapped themselves up in them.

As Nancy sat back to catch her breath she was able to fully appreciate the beautiful lake for the first time, until now her attention was completely focused on the nearest seat. The turquoise water shone as it lapped at the pebbles on the edge of the forest which they had just emerged from. It was bright and deep and echoed the particular shade of Torben's eyes.

"This is my favourite indsø." Torben nodded over to the lake. "We swim in here in the summer."

Although stunning, Nancy could tell it was almost freezing and shivered at the thought of plunging in now.

Suddenly pings and dings of all their mobile phones rang out as they picked up signal. Gleefully Tessa pawed through her bag to retrieve hers and then sat fully engrossed in catching up with two days' worth of unread messages and news. Even Torben glanced at his phone and a flash of surprise crossed his face.

Nancy was thoroughly enjoying being

101

completely cut off from society and had no intention of looking at hers, not even to check the time.

The waitress came over to take their order and brought with her some tiny glasses of schnapps. Nancy's eye was drawn to her beautiful red dress with exquisite embroidery on the front, a white blouse billowed underneath and a starched white apron finished the ensemble off.

"She looks amazing," said Nancy.

Looking up, Tessa agreed, "Yeah, that's cool!"

"Ah, that is our traditional dress," replied Torben. Looking at Tessa he said with a cheeky smile, "See, some old things are still relevant."

Tessa rolled her eyes with a grin and then returned promptly to her phone.

After clinking schnapps glasses and saying, "Skål," Torben then announced, "You must try the speciality here; the best smørrebrød in Denmark!"

"What are you signing us up for?" asked Neil cagily.

"Don't panic, it's like an open sandwich. I know how you English people like sandwiches. It's delicious, they catch the fish in the lake and smoke it here, it's beautifully fresh. And they put the tastiest prawns on top."

"Sounds amazing, sign me up," said Nancy.

The waitress delivered their lunch order and it looked spectacular. Hungry after their walk, they all dug in. Nancy was so enthusiastic she hadn't realised she had got some of the dill and mustard on her nose. Torben gently reached over and wiped it off, then kissed the spot where the sauce had rested. Their eyes met and Nancy felt so wonderfully content.

Torben's phone pinged again, breaking the spell. He glanced at the screen.

"It's work, sorry. I have to take this." He hurried off to make a phone call in private.

"You guys make me sick!" said Tessa, with a laugh. "You even make getting food on your face romantic!"

Nancy pretended to look offended. "At least one thing is going ok for me at the moment," she said. She had got carried away in the moment and suddenly all the angst about her job and her future came flooding back.

Torben returned after a short while, looking quite serious. "Nancy, will you come and walk with me to the lake?"

Nancy nodded, bemused and stood up. Torben tenderly picked up the blanket from her chair and wrapped it around her shoulders. Nancy remembered the magical snow storm they had watched on the hotel roof only a couple of days before. She couldn't believe how hard and fast she had fallen for Torben in such a short space of time. Their feet clacked on the stones of the shore and they made their way down to the very edge of the water.

Curiosity almost killing them, Tessa and Neil looked on. Neil had to pull Tessa onto his lap to stop her from getting up and moving closer to earwig.

Torben looked back over his shoulder to check they were a suitable distance away and would not be over heard. Nancy drew the blanket around closer, the chill from the lake starting to creep through her layers. The wind tugged at the tendrils of her hair.

"Is everything ok?" asked Nancy.

"Oh yes, well, I hope so. I have an unusual proposition for you."

"Go on," urged Nancy more than a little intrigued.

"I've just been speaking with George Lang, and he's offered me a promotion."

"Oh, that's fantastic. Well done," said Nancy, genuinely pleased for Torben, but unsure of how she came into it.

"He has developed a new role within the company; a hygge consultant." Torben laughed a little at this. "I kept trying to tell him that it doesn't translate, you can't just make hygge, but he is insisting that the world needs more hygge and that I am the man who can help."

"Hygge. What we were just talking

about? Being cosy and content with loved ones," mused Nancy. "Yes, the world definitely needs more of that."

"So, will you be my assistant? I need someone who believes in it as passionately as I do, and George and I can't think of anyone better than you."

"You mean as a job?"

"Yes, Junior Hygge Consultant with Danglish? Will you do it?" his serious face darkened further with intensity.

Elation coursed through her; she couldn't quite believe her luck. She quivered from her ear muffs all the way down to her snow boots. She threw her arms up and jumped to reach around Torben's neck pulling him down to her height. Kissing him passionately, her fingers curled into his hair. The red blanket caught dramatically in the wind and sailed up the bank; dancing and billowing with the gust.

"I would love that," she breathed.

"I would love it too," said Torben the boy-like light returning to his eyes. He plunged back down to kiss her further, harder and deeper. Tipping her over into a back bend.

Tessa and Neil were still looking on, clueless as to what was unfolding as they watched the couple stood on the water's edge.

Neil nudged Tessa and said, "Who knew that Torben had it in him?"

"Not me. I can't really believe it; Nancy and Torben."

"It's great though."

"Yes, but I feel bad, I think I judged him all wrong. Until Nancy, we never really did get on; I thought he was tedious and grouchy."

"I think he just needed to meet the right person."

"I'm so glad he has." Tessa looked over her shoulder to Neil and said, "I'm glad I have too."

Twisting round and leaning back she kissed him once on the lips. Not satisfied with that, Neil pulled her round to face him, readjusting her position on his lap. He kissed her fervently. His hands crept under her coat and jumper onto her soft warm skin and she gasped.

"Cold," she managed to say, while his lips consumed her.

"I'll warm you up," he replied.

The End

A Note from the Author

I hope you feel thoroughly warmed up by this winter novella. If you enjoyed it, please consider leaving a review on Amazon or Goodreads or any other review site. It doesn't have to be long and your comments would be very much appreciated. Reviews and feedback are vital to support independent authors so I cannot encourage you enough to not only leave a review for me but for any other books you read- thank you!

I'd love to hear from you, so please look out for me on Twitter (@S_JFraser) and Facebook (@sjfraserauthor).

Read on for an excerpt from The Spanish Indecision- book one in the Jenny Abroad series. Book two in the series is underway along with some other exciting projects.

Thanks for purchasing Candlelight and Snowball Fights and happy reading!

The Spanish Indecision –
a sample

If you enjoyed Candlelight and Snowball Fights you may enjoy a trip to Spain with my first novel, The Spanish Indecision. Here are the first few chapters. If you want to find out what happens it is available to purchase in paperback or as an e-book.

Chapter 1.

I stood in front of the mirror, still clutching my binder, drenched through to the skin. I couldn't shake the idea that Natalia had purposefully flipped the tray of drinks over me. Shivering a little pulled me out of my reverie.

"Something ought to fit," Pete had said as he gave me his locker key. I'd left him clearing up the mess; running off to a chorus of tuts and eye rolls from The Witches. For a bit of protection I'd grabbed my folder as I passed my desk, feeling like an entrant in a wet t-shirt competition.

The door squeaked and a waft of expensive aftershave puffed out of the locker as I opened it. Hanging up were some silk ties and two shirts; a blue and white striped double cuff and a plain white one. *Thank you, Pete!* I unhooked the white one and headed over to a changing cubicle.

I peeled off my shirt and found that my bra had been soaked through too. Wincing, I remembered the feeling of clunky mugs and scalding coffee raining down on me. Poking my head out of the cubicle, I checked the coast was clear before I rushed to the door and slid the bolt across. Feeling rather exposed I stood, naked from the waist up, wringing my bra out and holding it under the hand-dryer. For the first time ever I was pleased I had such a small chest-there wasn't too much material to dry.

The grunting started as I was hooking my bra back on. Wide eyed, I whipped around to see what was happening. My boss, Mr Thompson, and another man, quite frankly the most attractive man I've ever seen, suddenly shoulder barged through the door. *Why me? Why now? Why when I'm looking like this?*

With speed to rival an athlete I scuttled back into the cubicle, banging the door shut.

"Ah, sorry about that. We thought the door was stuck..." Mr Thompson explained.

I made an indistinguishable squeaking sound, humiliation choking me.

"So, ah, this is the staff room, where people mad enough to walk or cycle to work come and get changed," said Mr Thompson.

I could hear him giving the other man a tour as I rapidly tried to get some clothes on and recover a modicum of dignity.

Surprisingly, Pete's shirt looked ok once I had carefully tucked it in to my high waist, pencil skirt. I smoothed my hands over my blonde hair, although the slight headache from all the grips told me the large donut was still securely in place. Gathering up the ruined shirt and my organiser, I gingerly left the safety of the cubicle.

"Ah, young Jenny," said Mr Thompson.

I cringed. I hate it when people call me young. I was twenty-seven for goodness sake, but I looked about seventeen, and not in a 'you're ageing well' way, but in a 'you're clearly too young and inexperienced to have anything useful to add' kind of way. *And why did he say "ah" all the time?*

"This is...ah...Mr Henson, who will be your... ah...new line manager. He just transferred in from the ah... other branch," said Mr Thompson.

"Nice to meet you..." I trailed off, deciding to avoid using his name, sure I'd say handsome instead of Henson.

Clutching the coffee soaked shirt with one hand, I stuck out the other to Mr Henson, which he gave a firm shake. His eyes struck me first, steel blue and sparkling. His thick crop of dark brown hair was cut close at the sides and longer on top, there was a faint trace of stubble on his strong jaw. Deep creases around his mouth hinted at a nice smile, although his face was quite straight and serious. Hastily, I made my excuses and continued back to the office, feeling acutely mortified.

It was only when I was walking out of the staff room that I noticed the sign telling me that CCTV was in operation. *Oh no!* I thought of our resident security guards, Stan and Bill. Heat prickled my face as I pictured them huddled around their little TV screens, enjoying the show. I prayed that they'd been on a break as I pulled the door open and returned to my office.

The corridor was empty and as my cheeks cooled, thoughts of my gorgeous new boss floated around my head. I was sure that things were only going to get better at work. Surely, they couldn't get any worse?

Catching Pete's eye, I nodded what I hoped was a message of gratitude in his direction. As I sat down my eyes were drawn to the clock. Only three hours to go and I'd be jetting off to Spain with my best friend; I could barely contain my excitement as I thought of everything I'd arranged. It took a lot of effort, but I managed to drag my attention away from the hen do I'd planned for her, and focus on work.

Consulting the to-do list in my trusty

organiser, I let out a quiet huff of irritation as I looked over the first point.

REMEMBER YOU ARE OVER JAMES!

The less said about him the better. Lazy, arrogant, chauvinistic. He wasn't a nice guy and I could do so much better. The trouble was, I hadn't.

My mum was next on the list. Since her accident, I'd taken to worrying about her; our roles had suddenly been reversed. I typed a quick email to remind her I was going away and that I'd done an online food order for her. With Mum taken care of, I made myself feel better by scribbling down a few tasks I'd already completed- purely for the satisfaction of ticking them off. Feeling suitably productive, I decided I'd earned a break and went over to see Pete.

"You ok darling?" he asked as I got to his desk. He inclined his head over towards The Witches, reminding me of the coffee incident.

"Never better," I replied. I was aware that we were being observed and I didn't want to show any weakness.

He gave me a deep, understanding look and then said, "You're looking fabulous today, chick, you must give me the details of your designer!"

"Oh, I don't think you could afford him."

We chuckled and I felt some of the weight lift off my shoulders, it was so nice to have someone on my side. He's one of the nicest guys I've ever met. Shame he's in a very serious relationship with Jeremy from Finance.

Pete leaned in closer and whispered, "Don't go on holiday and leave me here with The Witches."

I laughed and said, "There's no chance I'm missing it, even for you!"

"I know," he replied and grinned. "You're gonna have such a fun time you know, now don't forget to go to "Breeze" the beach club and tell them that 'Posh Pete' sent you."

"POSH Pete?" I questioned.

"It's cos when I first went there they tried to ban me because I wasn't posh enough, darling, but they relented, oh how they relented." Pete sounded as if he had to overcome some sort of dramatic persecution and made a show of mock outrage.

"Ha! It sounds like they'll probably try and ban me too but we'll give it a go. I'm so excited about going to Spain, I've never been before."

"You'll have the best time! Are you all packed?"

"No, I'm leaving at lunch time today so I can go home and finish packing. I've got loads of holiday leave left so I thought I may as well use it. Actually, I best crack on and finish everything before I go."

"Hey, your legs look fab in those

heels," he called as I walked away.

The compliment gave me a lift and I headed back to my desk with a lighter heart.

Chapter 2.

The sound of The Witches quietly snickering drifted over to me as I typed up some minutes. Paranoid, I was sure it was about me.

"...Such a loser," I heard Natalia say.

She was the leader of the coven; Eve and Chantelle seem to worship her in a petrified kind of way. They all have dyed red hair and wear only black. I used to think they were all intimidating, now I've decided it's only Natalia who's terrifying.

Convinced they all hate me, my mind wandered. I hadn't been at this job long, about six months, but I had always had the sense that I didn't really belong here, and the bitchy girls had knocked my confidence. I didn't want to admit that it was a dead-end job, but truthfully, I couldn't see where I was going to be in six months' time. Being distracted with arranging the hen do probably wasn't helping.

More sniggering snapped me back to the present and I began typing up the minutes of that days meeting with renewed vigour. My work title was 'Office Assistant', it should have been 'PA' but I actually assisted all the managers in the office so there was nothing 'personal' about it. The moment I sent the finished document to email, my phone buzzed.

"Jenny George," I answered.

"Miss George, step into my office."

The phone clicked off before I could reply. It was unmistakably the new boss.

As I headed over to his office, I smoothed my skirt down against my hips. Aware that the first impression I had made was that of a startled, soggy loon who stunk of coffee, I resolved to make a better one this time.

I rapped my knuckles on the door and while I waited to be called in I began to wonder why I was being asked to see him. My ability to feel automatically guilty, regardless of whether I had done anything wrong, kicked in. *Maybe I was in trouble for work place nudity?*

My heart was pounding and I was certain that anyone nearby could hear it. By the time I was summoned in I was so nervous I had started to sweat; I was stewing in panic and angst.

As he shut the door I breathlessly babbled out, "I didn't know there was CCTV in the staff room. I didn't mean to cause offence to anyone I just needed to dry my bra."

Mr Henson raised his eyebrows, clearly taken aback. The word "bra" rang through my ears as I quickly realised being naked wasn't the reason I had been asked to see him. My face flushed and my previously thumping heart sank.

"Ahhh, thank you for that, Miss George, but that's not the reason I called you in here. Don't worry, you're not in trouble." His warm smile and gentle tone soon calmed me down. "I'm not even starting here properly until next week but I wanted to come in and familiarise myself with the staff and the office, and lay out some expectations so we all get off on the right foot. I'm going to be speaking to everyone individually like this."

His deep eyes met mine and the corners crinkled as he smiled. As I relaxed I let go of a deep breath.

"Ok." *Smooth line Jenny.*

With a welcoming gesture, he extended his arm out to the empty chair opposite his desk. I endeavoured to sit down elegantly without ruffling my carefully arranged outfit, I could feel his gaze burning into me, studying me. *He's probably thinking about my bra right now* I thought to myself. I had no idea how much he'd seen in the staff room and at that moment it felt like he was undressing me with his eyes.

"There're going to be some changes

around here. I'm going to be shuffling some things around. Everyone's output is going to be subject to review, it's a case of 'toe the line or get out'." He paused to chuckle at his cheesy metaphor, then continued, saying, "Which brings me to my first point, you should remember that personal emails are to be kept to a minimum. Perhaps you could send out a reminder of this to all staff, I know you are familiar with the process of sending out an email to multiple recipients." He gave me a coy grin as he said this.

Confused, I responded, "Yes, sir." *Really eloquent today Jenny.*

"And I'd like to get up to scratch with everything that's been happening as quickly as possible. So, I'd like the minutes from this morning's meeting to be typed up in the next hour so I can review what was discussed."

"Yes, Sir. About the minutes, I..."

"No excuses, Jenny," he said while drumming a pen on his desk. "You've got lots to be getting on with so I won't take up any more of your time."

He stood up and ushered me over to the door. As he held it open for me he reached out and engulfed my hand in his, giving it another good firm shake. My skin zinged from his unexpected touch.

He continued to hold my hand as he said, "I've got a good feeling about working here. I think we'll make a good team."

Warmth spread up from his strong grip as he gave me a final squeeze and then let me go. I could feel my cheeks pink up as I squeezed past him, inhaling the scent of cedar and mint as I brushed against his immaculately tailored suit. I smiled at the thought of what might be underneath; he was tall and built like a swimmer, all lean with broad shoulders.

As I headed back to my desk I did my best to repress the memory of babbling on at him about my underwear; if I didn't think about it, it didn't happen. Focusing instead on the bubble of excitement I could feel expanding inside me. A new face may shake things up around the place, and what a lovely new face it was too.

An image of my ex flashed through my mind briefly and I considered how different he was to James. It had been one year, three hundred days and two hours since he had broken my heart and walked out. I pushed all thoughts of him aside, and repeated to myself, *I deserve better than that, it's over.* I wondered if maybe, just maybe, Mr Henson might help me finish getting over him. It had been nearly two years and despite my best efforts, I hadn't managed to 'move on' or find someone else. As he was my senior, I was fully aware that absolutely nothing would happen between me and Mr Henson, but a girl can dream, surely?

Pete caught my eye and mouthed, "Everything alright?" across the office.

"Yes," I mouthed with a big goofy smile, and tried to beckon him over by waggling my eyebrows.

"You seem more upbeat, I think I know what's put a spring in your step!" he said when he arrived.

"So, I've met our new boss, he seems...like a good addition," I said, picking my words carefully. Then lowering my voice, I added, "I totally embarrassed myself earlier but he was so nice about it."

"He was totally flirting with you! I was watching him fawn over you as you walked out the office," Pete told me, leaning in, his eyes dancing. "You must have done something right, he seemed a bit stern to me. He gave a speech about things changing around here and that he ran a tight ship and such while you were out of the room. He seems to like a metaphor that one."

"No, he seemed lovely. He had some suggestions for me, but nothing that I can't handle. I've done half of it already."

A flicker of panic passed over me, *I had sent the minutes, hadn't I?* I checked my computer. Yes, I had. And there below it was my email to my mum, with the words "send to all contacts" written in the recipients' column. A feeling of sickness passed over me, who needs Natalia to embarrass me when I was doing a perfectly good job of humiliating myself today?

I looked to Pete and pretended to bury my head in my hands.

"Oh, don't you worry about that email; we've all done something like that before. Natalia once sent out her online order of diet pills to the whole office, it's easily done."

I stifled a snigger, not wanting to draw any more attention to myself.

Everything Mr Henson had said to me suddenly made sense. "Now I know what he was talking about, I've made such a prat of myself."

"No, you haven't and anyway, you're one of the best workers we've got here; he'll soon see that."

"I best get back to work and try and leave the new boss with a good third impression before I go off to Spain."

Pete laughed and said, "Absolutely, the first and second ones are overrated anyway. Now, you have a fab time, darling, and we'll do lunch when you're back, yeah?"

"Looking forward to it already," I said, truthfully.

He gave me a big hug before he headed back to his desk.

A message pinged up on my phone and I smiled when I saw it was from Kirsty.

[YO! HEAD BRIDESMAID, ARE YOU READY TO

PARRRRRTY?! K X]

She's a bit bonkers but I love her. We've been best friends since we met in secondary school and bonded over our mutual love for a too embarrassing to mention boyband and us both having a mortal fear of sewing machines and other textile related equipment. We've been pretty inseparable ever since. Not wanting to miss a chance to wind her up, I fired back:

[There's no need to shout. Now, what's all this about a bridesmaid and partying? Is someone getting married? I was planning a quiet weekend doing some knitting, did you have something else in mind? Xx]

[EEEEEEEP! NOW I KNOW YOU'RE JOKING, YOU CAN'T KNIT FOR SH!#. HEN DOOOOO WOOP WOOP! XXXXXXXXXXXX]

Chuckling to myself, I tossed my phone aside and then turned my attention back to work. Diligently ploughing through the rest of the to-do list so I didn't implode with excitement about my holiday. With great satisfaction, I set my automatic email reply to say that I would be out of the office and then strode out, only looking back to smile at Pete.

As I passed the security desk in the foyer I got a little cheer from Stan and Bill. Rolling my eyes, I gave them a mini bow like an actress at the end of her performance, figuring that getting all flustered about it would only keep them entertained longer. I bumped in to Mr Henson again as I got to the doors.

"Miss George," he said by way of greeting, nodding slightly to me. His smouldering gaze locked on to mine.

"Hello, Mr Henson." I struggled not to seem overwhelmed by his powerful good looks as I scurried by. The heat from his stare followed me as I walked away...

***

Read on for some reviews to see what some people are saying about The Spanish Indecision:

☆☆☆☆☆ Just great!! I loved it!

Absolutely loved this! I didn't want to put it down, always something happening and a great twist at the end. An easy-to-read book, really enjoyable...I can't wait to read the next novel and see what lies ahead for Jenny.

☆☆☆☆☆ Throw an umbrella in your cocktail and start reading!

Sarah-Jane Fraser will take you to the sun, the beach, the culture and the boys of Spain in her debut book. A fun, feel-good read that celebrates friendship, loyalty, and the hallmarks of life and love. With relatable characters and an unexpected plot twist, you have a story that you can't put down until the very last page. This book is the perfect accompaniment to sipping a cocktail on a warm summer evening while dreaming of travelling abroad. Looking forward to the continuation of the series!

☆☆☆☆☆ **Well written, light-hearted read**

The Spanish indecision is a well written, fun and light-hearted read. Unlike some holiday reads, I really cared about the characters - especially Jenny - and I enjoyed the authentic Spanish references. Funny but not silly, romantic but tasteful, easy to read but not predictable - I can't wait to find out where Jenny goes next! (I received an ARC of this book in exchange for an honest review)

☆☆☆☆☆ **Loved it! Takes you straight to sunny Spain - a first class holiday read**

The Spanish Indecision is a brilliant summer read that encapsulates perfectly that holiday feeling – it took me right back to holidays and good times with my girlfriends.

I loved the balance of intrigue (I didn't guess the twist) and humour (I laughed out loud a LOT) and really enjoyed getting to know the characters, especially the ones I loved to hate. I cannot wait to find out what's next for Jenny... (I received an ARC of this book in exchange for an honest review).

☆☆☆☆☆ Witty Chick Book - A Must For Your Summer Holiday!

Fab first book from Sarah-Jane Fraser...the characters had me hooked from the start...I laughed, was curious, felt anxious for the main character so simply had to read on to find out the ending - no spoilers from me. All the characters were very charming. The only thing that was missing for me was the actual sea and sun to be reading it in - superb holiday read. I received an ARC of this book in exchange for an honest review.

☆☆☆☆☆ A charming book that will make you smile

If you are looking for an easy read that will transport you from everyday life, then look no further. The characters are very relatable and likeable, elements are sure to make you reflect on your own friendships which let's face it, is always heartwarming. Some parts made me genuinely chuckle, I read the entire thing on a long train journey and I can honestly say it made the whole ordeal forgotten as I emersed myself in this sunny happy story. A charming little book that will stick a smile on your face.

☆☆☆☆☆ I loved it!

I loved it! Jenny is so likeable and relatable - I was in no doubt that I wanted her to have a happy ending! Definite recommendation for a great summer read.

Printed in Great Britain
by Amazon